SILVER ISLAND MOON

MAUI ISLAND SERIES BOOK 2

KELLIE COATES GILBERT

PRAISE FOR KELLIE'S BOOKS

∼

"If you're looking for a new author to read, you can't go wrong with Kellie Coates Gilbert."

~**Lisa Wingate**, NY Times bestselling author of *Before We Were Yours*

"Well-drawn, sympathetic characters and graceful language"

~**Library Journal**

"Deft, crisp storytelling"

~**RT Book Reviews**

"Gilbert's heartfelt fiction is always a pleasure to read."

~**Buzzing About Books**

Copyright © 2021 by Kellie Coates Gilbert

All rights reserved.

No part of this book may be reproduced in any form or by any electronic or mechanical means, including information storage and retrieval systems, without written permission from the author, except for the use of brief quotations in a book review.

Silver Island Moon is a work of fiction. Names, characters, places, and incidents are either the product of the author's imagination or are used factiously, and any resemblance to actual persons, living or dead, is coincidental.

Cover Design: Elizabeth Mackay

*This book is dedicated to Jaslyn Ausmus.
You will always be my baby girl.*

ALSO BY KELLIE COATES GILBERT

THE MAUI ISLAND SERIES
Under The Maui Sky

THE PACIFIC BAY SERIES
Chances Are

Remember Us

Chasing Wind

Between Rains

THE SUN VALLEY SERIES
Sisters

Heartbeats

Changes

Promises

LOVE ON VACATION SERIES
Otherwise Engaged

All Fore Love

TEXAS GOLD SERIES
A Woman of Fortune

Where Rivers Part

A Reason to Stay

What Matters Most

STAND ALONE NOVELS

Mother of Pearl

Available at all retailers

www.kelliecoatesgilbert.com

SILVER ISLAND MOON
MAUI ISLAND SERIES, BOOK 2

Kellie Coates Gilbert

1

Christel Briscoe tossed her remaining coffee into the sink and placed her favorite mug inside the dishwasher. She glanced at her watch with alarm, knowing the extra minutes in bed this morning had cost her. If she wanted to beat traffic, she'd better get moving. Her sister, Katie, might waltz into work whenever she deemed to show up, but being prompt and on time was essential. Time mattered, and she didn't waste it.

After a quick shower, she pulled her blow dryer from her bathroom drawer and dried her short blonde hair. With this last cut, she'd taken the advice of her stylist and gone shorter in the back leaving the front and sides a little longer. Trying to replicate her stylist's skills, she squeezed a dollop of product into her palm and worked it through her hair, giving the style a chunky look.

When she'd finished, she leaned into the mirror and gazed at her reflection. She had to admit, she liked this new look. At almost thirty-five, she didn't want to be one of those women who were afraid to try new things.

Besides, change was good. She'd been in a bit of a funk. The last six months had been hard. No, not just hard. Her father's passing and the discovery of his affair with a close family friend had shaken Christel to her core, left her feeling unsteady. She was a lawyer. She liked black and white rules. Gray areas were never her comfort zone.

Unfortunately, life rarely cooperated.

Christel grabbed her bag and headed for the door, determined to shake off the past. She vowed to take the advice of her mother, a woman she admired. One small crack did not mean the family was broken. It meant they had been put to the test and didn't fall apart.

As she opened her car door her cell phone buzzed. It was probably Katie, she thought as she dug inside her bag. Her sister seemed to have an insatiable need to chat while drinking her morning coffee.

Christel pulled out her phone to find a meeting notification. A meeting she'd completely spaced.

"Crud!" She tossed her bag on the passenger seat and folded into the driver's seat. She had less then fifteen minutes to drive to Pali Maui, their family's pineapple plantation. A drive that normally would take a half hour, in good traffic. She swallowed hard as she started the engine.

"Hey," Maggie Donovan called out as Christel pulled from the driveway. Her neighbor wore a bright pink jogging suit with matching running shoes and waved her arms wildly.

Christel lived in a trendy residential enclave known as Maui by the Sea. Her neighbors were mostly affluent career-driven couples with children. She was only one of a few singles, which included Maggie, an older widow, who walked religiously every morning.

Christel groaned and lowered her window. "Hey, Maggie. Look, I'm really running late."

"Oh, poo. Young people hurry far too much. When you get to be my age, you realize there's value in slowing down a bit. Life is too short to miss the moments."

"I—I have a meeting." Christel didn't want to be rude, but she didn't have a minute to spare. Maggie was known for grabbing far more than a minute in these encounters.

"Okay, I'll let you go." Maggie pushed her sunglasses up into her white hair. "First, you have to promise to join me for a little dinner party. I met this really nice young man at the bank the other day. He just moved to the island and he needs to meet people. The best part? He's a doctor."

In Maggie speak, that meant her neighbor was set on connecting her single next-door neighbor with another prospect. Maggie had been trying to hook her up ever since the divorce. Like she was ready for all that again.

"That's so sweet, Maggie. I'll tell you what, let me check my calendar when I get to work and see when I might squeeze in something." She looked at her neighbor apologetically. They both knew it would be a freezing cold day in Maui before she'd agree to that dinner. Blind dates were one of those gray areas she hated. "I really have to go, Maggie." To further make her point, she waved and raised her window before backing out onto the street. Minutes later, she pulled out of the neighborhood onto the highway and gunned it. She gripped the steering wheel. *Let's see what this Miata can do.*

Christel was barely on the outskirts of Pa'ia when she heard a siren wailing behind her. She quickly glanced in the rearview mirror to find red lights blaring on a police car as the vehicle drew near.

Her foot immediately lifted from the accelerator. An adrenaline rush kicked in as she slowed and pulled off the road. Crud! Crud!

With her heart pounding, she cut the engine and grabbed

her wallet from her purse. She'd never been issued a citation. Guess there was a first time for everything.

Christel watched a police officer in full uniform exit his patrol car. He marched to her passenger door and motioned for her to lower the window.

She immediately complied. "Sorry, Officer. Was I speeding?" What a stupid question. Of course, she was speeding. Her nerves were getting the best of her. She granted the officer her widest smile in hopes of gaining favor.

It was then that she recognized his face. "Web? Webley Green?"

One of her former schoolmates from high school smiled back at her. "Hey, you remember me."

Remember him? Who could forget Webley Green? He was one of the strangest kids she'd ever known. While most of the class dressed in shorts and flip-flops, Web wore an old army surplus jacket everywhere he went. And John Lennon-type glasses. His hair was carrot orange, and he was tall and lanky, like a new baby colt who had yet to grow into his wobbly legs.

Web had asked her to the prom and she'd declined. She'd felt bad after seeing the disappointment on his face. But go to the prom with Webley Green? Uh, no.

Christel forced a smile. "Of course, I remember you, Webley. How have you been? I'm a little surprised to see you. I heard you moved off island after school."

He puffed out his chest. "Yes, I did. Went to the University of Washington. Got a criminal justice degree. And, well, here I am...a proud member of the Pa'ia police force. I'm currently a highway patrol officer. But I've got my eyes set on becoming a detective. Per my training," he quickly added.

The sun caught his badge. The glint made her blink. "Well, that's...impressive." She didn't dare look at her watch, but there was no doubt now she was going to miss her meeting. She'd have to text her mother and ask her to cover. Something she hated to do. Mom had enough on her plate.

"Thanks," he said, unable to contain his smile. "I like it. What about you? What are you doing these days?"

After a quick glance at the citation book in his hands, she raised her gaze level with his. "I'm a lawyer. I work for my family." She briefly updated him on her mom and siblings and on Pali Maui and how the business had grown, intentionally skipping the part about her dad.

Web slipped the citation book into his back pocket, bent and leaned his arms on the door. Through the open window, he grinned. "Say, I was wondering...I mean, I see you aren't wearing a ring." He looked to her left hand. "And a while back, I was browsing an online dating site. Imagine my surprise when your face showed up. Your profile said you liked a good brunch. So, I was thinking...why don't you let me take you to the Four Seasons this weekend. They have a great Sunday buffet. Unless you go to church. I mean, we could go to church together first. Whatever you want."

The color drained from Christel's face. She was going to kill her sister! She'd told her to take that profile down and never do something like that again. Why was everyone always trying to fix her up? She was just fine remaining single. Men were nothing but trouble.

"Oh, I don't think so." She scrambled to think of some excuse. "I...well, my dad passed away not so long ago and I'm still not up for any kind of socializing right now." Epic new low. Now she was using her dad as an excuse? She'd sold her soul to the devil.

Web's face filled with sympathy. He placed his hand on her arm. "I hadn't heard. That's awful. I am so sorry."

Christel attempted to manufacture sadness. "Yeah, life is short. We need to enjoy all the moments."

He nodded and slowly lifted his hand from her. "So true.

Well, look...you've obviously had a lot on your mind. Let me just issue you a warning. And about that date, I absolutely understand. We can give it a few weeks."

She thanked him profusely and handed over her driver's license and car registration, purposely ignoring the last comment.

Web took her license and registration and promised to be right back. He sauntered to his vehicle, leaned inside, and grabbed the radio, and spoke to someone. When he noticed her watching, he waved and gave her a reassuring nod.

When he returned, he had the warning made out. "Be careful," he cautioned, handing the slip of paper to her. "I'd hate to see you get in an accident." He passed over her driver's license and registration. "Like I said, I'll call you," he added with a slight grin.

His cell phone rang and he pulled it to his ear. "Yeah, Officer Green here." He held up a finger signaling her to hold on a minute while he listened. Web nodded somberly. "Got it."

He shoved his phone into his pocket. "Look, I've got to go. There's been a boat explosion in Kahului Bay. Multiple injuries." His eyes widened and he barely bid her goodbye before he rushed for his patrol car.

Her phone buzzed on the seat next to her. Christel picked it up. It was her sister.

"Hey, Katie. Look, I thought I told you to take my profile down from that online dating site—"

"Christel," Katie interrupted. "There's been an explosion. We just got word Aiden was on a boat that blew up. He's been hurt and they're taking him to Maui Memorial. Meet us there." Katie clicked off without waiting for a response.

Christel stared at her phone for several seconds letting the news sink in. She tossed her cell back on the passenger seat. With her heart painfully thumping against her chest, she hit the ignition and punched the accelerator, barely checking for oncoming traffic before pulling back onto the highway.

Her brother was hurt.

Nothing...and she meant, *nothing*, was going to stop her from getting to him.

2

Maui Memorial Medical Center was located in Wailuku, nearly forty minutes away by car, even with no traffic. Christel remarkably made the trip in fifteen.

She pulled off Mahalani Street and aimed her car for the front portico before screeching to a stop at the entrance. She scrambled from inside and tossed her keys into the hands of the parking attendant. "Emergency," she yelled over her shoulder, not bothering to wait for her claim ticket.

Christel's foot tapped impatiently as she waited for the glass entry doors to slide open. When they finally did, she had to sidestep around an elderly man in a wheelchair and the curt nurse pushing him through the front doors. She mumbled, "Excuse me," and darted inside.

The lobby was large with walls of glass offering a view of a stand of palms and three flag poles. Christel quickly scanned the lobby searching for the front desk. Although she'd been here many times, in her panic she couldn't seem to focus.

Spotting the desk on the far side of the sun-dappled lobby, Christel hurried forward, stopping in front of a woman with a round face and deep dimples. "My brother. They brought him here. Aiden Briscoe?"

The woman took her sweet time looking up from her computer screen. "I'm sorry. Who are you looking for?"

"A boating accident," Christel nearly shouted. "My brother. They brought him here."

Recognition dawned. "Oh my, yes. I heard about that." She pointed down a corridor. "The emergency department is down there. Turn left at the end of the hallway."

"Thanks," Christel said, then broke into a sprint making her way in that direction.

The emergency waiting room was packed but no sign of Katie, or her mother and Shane. Unnerved, she pulled out her phone and went to text when she heard Shane call out. "Christel."

She turned and rushed for him. "Where is he? Is Aiden okay?"

He looked at her, and in a single glance, they communicated perfectly. The family had suffered enough loss. They couldn't lose Aiden, too.

"He's alive. But he's pretty messed up. They just took him upstairs to the surgical floor. Mom told me to wait for you." He grabbed her elbow and pulled her to an elevator. The doors opened and a young woman chased after a toddler, who stayed steps ahead of his tired-looking mother. Shane and Christel got in the elevator and Shane punched the button. The doors closed and the elevator chugged upward.

"Do you know what happened?" Christel asked.

Shane ran his hand through the top of his hair. It was then that she noticed he had on his board shorts and a shirt that was buttoned wrong. "All I know is that he responded to a mayday from some vessel. They got the few passengers off but before Aiden could finish up, the thing exploded."

Christel felt the air leave her chest. Around her the tiny

elevator closed in. "Exploded," she echoed. "Is he—Is he burned?"

Shane shook his head. "Not that I heard. I didn't get to see him. They worked on him for several minutes before taking him up. Said it was critical they do some scans to see what was going on inside. He suffered some broken bones, I know that." Tears pooled in his eyes and he angrily brushed them aside. "I think he'll be okay."

Christel heard the words, but the look on her younger brother's face as he ducked his head suggested another outcome.

Shane looked up from rebuttoning his shirt. "What?" he said when he saw his sister staring. "I was in a hurry."

The elevator doors opened to a small waiting room lined with stiff wooden chairs with blue seat cushions. There was a television mounted on the wall, blaring news of the accident. Her family was gathered by the vending machine, obviously too upset to sit.

Christel moved for them. "Mom?"

While middle-aged, her mother was still a beautiful woman with her dark-brown hair curled slightly at her jaw. She looked twenty years younger than her fifty-five years. But today her green eyes were dull and her usually tanned complexion was ashen. In the past year, she'd been through hell and back. She'd lost her husband, then learned of his affair with a family friend. Now this. When she opened her arms to Christel, she teetered. Shane put a steadying hand on his mother.

"He's going to be all right," Mom quickly assured them all. "He's injured but not critical. The scans will tell us more." Ava pulled her daughter into an embrace. "They've called in an orthopedic specialist."

Christel glanced at the others. "Did anyone get to see him?"

"We did," Katie answered, joining them. Jon held little Noelle. She leaned over his shoulder and pointed to the candy she'd eyed in the vending machine. "I want some dum. Can I have some dum?" She opened and closed her chubby little fingers while stretching toward the glass front machine where a pack of green-packaged Doublemint waited.

"Not right now, baby," he told her. Her face filled with disappointment. She frowned and stuck her thumb in her mouth in response.

Katie pulled her phone from her bag. "I need to call Willa and update her. She's with a friend."

"Shh...listen." Shane pointed to the television, where scenes of a mangled boat floated in the ocean, smoke billowing from what must have been the engine room.

"*Here's what we know so far,*" the anchor reported into the microphone. "*Multiple passengers were taken to Maui Memorial Medical Center following an explosion on board a tour boat in Kahalui Bay that occurred at approximately ten o'clock this morning. One victim is reported to be in stable condition, and the other was treated and released,*" he said. "*A third victim, a member of the rescue unit, was more severely injured, and we are waiting to learn the extent of his injuries.*"

The screen cut back to images of the half-emerged boat. "*Coast Guard officials at the scene reported stable ocean conditions had quickly turned windy leaving the boat experiencing engine trouble and unable to return to shore. Maui Emergency Services responded to the scene and conducted the rescue. It's unwise at this point to speculate exactly what happened and why, but eye witnesses on shore report they saw the stalled boat and spotted smoke just before the explosion,*" the voice over told them. "*The Kiele V boat, owned by a local tourist company, did cruises, taking passengers off the east side of Maui to spot humpback whales.*"

The camera returned to the anchor. "*We are deeply saddened by this accident, and our concern is for those who have been affected by this tragic event.*"

"All we can do now is wait," their mom said.

. . .

The minutes drug into hours while the Briscoe family sat in those hospital chairs drinking stale coffee and hoping for news. The wait was interrupted by a stern voice coming over PA. "Paging Dr. Mickelson. Paging Dr. Mickelson."

A woman with a stethoscope draped around her neck entered from behind two automated doors at the end of the hallway. As she saw the family members and their worried faces, her expression turned sympathetic. "Mrs. Briscoe?" she asked Ava.

Ava popped up from her seat. "Yes?"

"It looks like your son suffered no life-threatening internal injuries. Beyond a bruised spleen, he's remarkably unscathed." She paused letting the information sink in. "He did sustain fractures to his right femoral shaft and ankle. These injuries are going to require surgery. They are prepping him now."

Ava's hand went to her throat. "Can we see him."

The nurse shook her head. "I'm afraid not. He's been sedated to relieve the pain. We'll be wheeling him back in moments." She held up a clip board. "Now, I'll need a main contact person from his immediate family. That would be you?"

Ava nodded. She pulled the pen from the nurse's fingers and filled out her name and cell number. When finished, she handed the clipboard and pen back. "We'll be right here, though. We're not leaving until he's out of surgery and okay."

The nurse smiled. "Of course. We'll add your cell to our system so you can call back and see how the surgery is going."

"Oh. Okay. How long do you expect the surgery to take?"

"Several hours," the nurse reported. "I'd suggest you might go get something to eat. We have a cafeteria. The food isn't restaurant quality, but it's good."

Ava shook her head. "Thank you, but no. Like I said, I'm not leaving."

The nurse hugged the clipboard to her chest and offered a commiserative smile. "We're good at what we do. Our surgeons are topnotch."

Ava nodded. "Still, I want to be here. Close."

Christel and Katie followed suit. They moved to their mother's side. "We're staying, too."

Jon patted Noelle's back as she laid her head on his shoulder, her eyes growing heavy. "If you take her, I'll go get all of us some food," he suggested.

Katie extracted her daughter from his arms and dropped into a nearby chair. "Man, she's getting heavy."

The wait began again. This time in earnest. The hands on the wall clock seemed to inch forward at the speed of a slow creeping lava flow.

"Call them, Mom," Christel urged. "It's been an hour and the nurse said it was okay for you check in occasionally."

Just as Ava was lifting her phone, it buzzed. Christel stretched over her mom's shoulder to see—unknown caller. Moments ticked by as she listened.

When Ava finally hung up, Christel was about to explode. "What did they say?"

Her mom's voice was shaky, but calm. "They're repairing some of the damage now—concentrating on the femoral injury. He's doing well. They should be finishing up within the hour. The nurse said she'd call with an update when she can."

Christel buried her attention in her phone where she researched orthopedic techniques and recovery times for Aiden's injuries. Like always, there seemed to be conflicting information. One respected medical site said healing time could extend into months, with even more months of rehab.

Aiden would not like that. His job was everything to him. Being laid up and unable to do what he loved would be hard to take. Then there was the fact he couldn't live on his own without some sort of help, at least in the near interim.

Katie seemed to have come to the same conclusion on her own. "You know, Aiden is not going to be able to remain at his house. He'll have to move in with one of us."

"He'll move home," Ava stated plainly as she gathered empty bags and food wrappers from Jon's trip to the cafeteria. "With me."

"I have a feeling he's going to be in the hospital for a good while," Jon offered. "I broke my wrist playing football in high school. It took forever to heal. Aiden's injuries are much more extensive. That leg break may require traction."

A noise from down the hall caught their attention. They all looked up to find Ava's best friend, Alani, and her husband, Elta, heading in their direction. They were followed by Mig Nakamoa, their farm manager at Pali Maui. Behind him, there was no mistaking the next person—their uncle, a burly bear of a man everyone on the island knew as Captain Jack.

The group hit the waiting room like a swarm of buzzing bees, talking over the top of each other while asking questions.

Ava finally interrupted the barrage by holding up open palms. "Okay, we should know something more soon. Until then, let's just be thankful his life was spared."

"Yes, the Lord is good," Elta said. He was the pastor of Wailea Chapel and tended to see everything through spiritual eyes.

"How are you, sweet thing?" Alani took Ava's hand and squeezed.

Ava's eyes teared up. "I'm just so thankful it wasn't worse."

Alani drew her into an embrace. "Oh, honey. Me, too."

Jack scowled. "Word has it that rig has been running into trouble for months. You can't ignore engine issues. They can turn about and bite your butt faster than a whitetip reef shark."

Ava put a hand on her brother's hairy arm as a silent message.

"Oh, sorry. Pardon the colorful language." He stroked his

bushy gray beard and gave everyone an apologetic look before adding, "I'm just saying."

In all the commotion, they nearly missed seeing a man with graying hair at the temples enter the waiting room wearing blue scrubs. He was followed by two women, one with a clipboard and deep-set eyes that scanned the room, taking inventory of those seated and waiting for information.

He cleared his throat. "Excuse me. I'm Dr. Evan Matisse, Aiden's surgeon."

All talking immediately ceased. Ava and Christel simultaneously moved for him. "Doctor?" Ava said, her voice revealing how grueling the wait had been for her.

"Let's everybody take a seat."

The doctor pulled his surgical cap from his head. "First, Aiden is out of danger. At least for now. Femoral breaks like his can be gnarly and cause havoc with the circulatory system. So, it's always important that these situations be remedied as quickly as possible."

Ava buried her head against her brother's shoulder. Jack patted her arm, his eyes filled with relief.

"And the surgery?" Christel ventured.

"This surgery was fairly arduous and will be one of several before we're through. We've placed an intermedullary rod to stabilize the femoral break and did what we could to repair the structural damage to his knees. He had a torn meniscus and damaged ligaments. The ankle repair will happen tomorrow. We don't like having patients anesthetized for long periods of time when we can help it." He drew a deep breath. "Aiden is young. He's strong and otherwise healthy. While the road to full recovery will be a challenge and will take time, I have every reason to believe he will get through this and will eventually be walking like normal, barring complications."

"How much time?" Shane asked, voicing the question running through everyone's mind.

"That can depend on a number of factors. But likely we're talking months," the doctor told them.

Ava reached for Christel. "Can we see him?"

Christel turned to face the doctor. Their gaze met, and he gave her a tired smile. She guessed him to be in his mid-forties. He had a precisely trimmed beard and mustache that matched the color of his thick hair. His eyes were light green with a gray tint that reminded her of the color of the ocean when storms rolled in. He was a giant in her eyes—a savior of sorts. The one who had taken a dire situation and had performed medical magic.

She returned the smile.

In that brief moment, emotion rolled over Christel like ocean waves pounding the shoreline. In the end, Aiden was going to be fine.

"You coming?" Katie asked, pulling at her arm.

"Yeah." Christel couldn't help herself. In relief, she flung her arms around the doctor's broad shoulders. "Thank you for taking care of my brother. You don't know—" She let her voice fade.

He gently patted her on the back. "I do know."

She pulled away and looked at him, allowed a timid smile. It was as if in that split moment, he knew her. He saw into her soul.

"C'mon," Katie demanded.

Christel reluctantly bid her newfound hero goodbye and followed her family down a hall and through a large circular area. In the center was a nurses' station with bleeping monitors mounted on the counter. Beyond were individual areas cordoned off by glass walls. Those with patients were dimly lit. Some were darkened and had empty beds, neatly made up for the next people unfortunate enough to need them.

Finally, they came to a stop.

Beyond the glass, her unconscious brother was positioned

in a bed. His leg was suspended midair with a steel bar and chains. The ankle was wrapped with ice packs. Machines with blinking lights stood sentinel on either side of the hospital bed and an IV dripline was attached to one of his hands.

Their mother rushed to his side, bent and gently wiped a strand of perspiration pasted hair from his forehead. "Oh, baby."

The sight tightened Christel's chest. But not in a bad way. In that moment, she was more than grateful. Aiden had suffered an accident that had left them all reeling. In the end, he was going to be all right. The recovery would, no doubt, be long and arduous. While difficult, her brother would do the required work and regain his physical abilities in full.

Especially with his family by his side.

3

"Let's go! Let's go!" Captain Dennis hollered as he pushed another boat passenger into the waiting arms of Grant Hogan, Aiden's fellow emergency response specialist. The frightened woman glanced back over her shoulder to make sure her husband was following behind her.

His stomach filled with adrenaline as Aiden placed his hand on the man's wrinkled, age-spotted arm, guiding him across the deck of the boat and handing him off to Grant, who helped him into the waiting rescue boat. His wife embraced him and they took their place on the crowded vessel, huddled together.

Captain Dennis leaned against the railing of the damaged tour boat. A wave hit the side of the boat and the vessel listed dangerously. Dennis changed his focus and pointed in the direction of the cabin. "Move!" he shouted. "Now, Briscoe!"

Aiden glanced to where the captain pointed. Dark smoke billowed into the air. His heart pounded as he hollered back, "One last check." He scrambled a couple of yards across the deck. "All clear!" he shouted.

Captain Dennis waved for him to hurry, and he raced in that direction.

Before Aiden made it halfway to his captain, he felt the blast. A searing heat accompanied by immediate pain as the force of an explosion catapulted him forward then slammed him onto the deck. It felt as if every limb of his body were tearing away from the joints. The impact felt like a slab of cement slamming into his back, the intense heat.

Then, the darkness...

"Aiden? Time to wake up. C'mon, let's open those eyes."

Aiden's forehead broke into a cold sweat. He cracked his eyes open to bright blinding light.

"There he is," a female voice said.

He opened his eyes a little wider, winced as his foggy brain cleared.

A nurse?

Aiden bolted up only to have his shoulders caught by the two women flanking the metal railing on his bed. "Shhh...calm down. You're fine," one said, gently pressing him back against the white pillow.

His mouth was dry as cotton. "Where...where am I?" he pushed out, his voice raspy and distant, even to his own ears.

"You're in Maui Memorial Medical Center. You've just come out of surgery."

"Surgery?" he asked, lifting his hand to his pounding forehead. His vision blurred then cleared again.

"Whoa, be careful," the nurse said, catching his hand. "You have an IV."

Aiden looked and confirmed what she said was true. He scowled as his vision cleared even more. Fragments of memory formed.

He was in an accident. An explosion. On the boat.

Frantic, he tried to sit up again. Then he realized his leg was in a cast and suspended from a metal bar floating several feet above the bed. "What the—"

Beyond the glass wall, a nurses' station buzzed with activity. His mother immediately appeared in the doorway, her face etched with worry.

"He's awake," the nurse reported. "But I can already tell this one is going to be trouble." She gave Aiden a wink.

His mother rushed to his side, bent and gently wiped a strand of perspiration pasted hair from his forehead. "Oh, baby."

Christel, Katie, and Shane clamored close behind.

The nurse motioned for them to wait outside. "Let's give him a moment."

A prickling of anxiety trickled up his spine and lit his brain. He was injured. Bad.

"Mom. Tell me...what happened?"

Her soothing touch calmed him as she caressed his stubbled cheek. "You were in an accident, honey. An explosion."

Yes, he remembered.

"You were hurt," she told him.

He swallowed against the dryness in his throat. "How bad?" He closed his eyes, waited for the edict.

"The impact of the explosion threw you several feet. You landed hard. You fractured your right femur in two places. They've placed a rod to help heal the break. Your right knee is also injured...a torn meniscus and damaged ligaments. Your ankle is also badly sprained, but no fractures. In the morning, they'll perform a second surgery to help repair those issues."

"Internally?" he queried, knowing the injuries you couldn't see can often be the worst.

His mom shook her head. "The surgeon assured us you only sustained a bruised spleen. No internal bleeding. No rips or tears to any organs." She couldn't seem to help it. Her eyes welled with tears. "You're going to be fine. In no time, you'll be back to walking."

He stared at her intently trying to let her words register. When they did, they hit with the force of a blow. Injuries of that extent would impact him for a long while. Surgeries, recovery and rehab. The road ahead would be a long one.

Aiden sat quietly as he watched his life pass before his eyes. Everything was going to be different. And not just for a few weeks. His life. The life he knew. Was over.

He fought back the hopelessness, working the muscle in his jaw to keep from breaking down. What about work? What about surfing? Dating? Riding a motorcycle? All gone for the foreseeable future.

He drew several deep breaths trying to put things into perspective. When he did, he realized he was lucky. Things could've been so much worse. Somehow the thought did little to comfort the puncture to his soul.

Aiden wanted to give his mother a reassuring smile, but there was no smile inside him right now. He knew what all this meant. None of it good.

His mom saw his fear, his uncertainty. "You'll be good as new," she assured him again, her lip quivering and her hand searching for somewhere to pat his arm. Her hand hung there between them for a few moments before she finally dropped it. "It may take a while, but all of this will soon be behind you. You'll see. Until then, you'll move in with me. After you leave the hospital, that is."

"And the others? Captain Dennis and the rest?"

"All are going to be fine. Only minor injuries. Captain Dennis suffered a sprained shoulder. He's already been treated and released." She paused, her hazel eyes narrowing. "Listen to me, son. The team's efforts were heroic, including yours. Lives were saved. Everyone is already expressing their gratitude."

Her assurances did little to raise his spirits. He tried to sit up again, but the needle in his vein resisted, sending a spike of pain shooting up his arm. Muttering a curse, he ignored the pinching and positioned himself so he could see better.

"Oh, honey. Please be careful," his mother cautioned. "You just woke up from surgery." She looked to the nurse, who stood checking one of the monitors, for support.

The nurse nodded. "Yes, you need to stay still. Let that anesthesia work out of your system."

His siblings could wait no longer. Ignoring the nurse's earlier caution, they pressed through the doorway and made their way to his bedside.

"How are you feeling?" Christel asked, placing her hand on his arm.

"Dude, you scared us!" Shane told him.

Katie leaned and gave his cheek a light kiss. "I'm so glad you're all right."

All right was a relative term. Was it all right that he would be laid up for months? Unable to work and do what he loved? All right that he had to move back in with his mother?

He swallowed against the thick lump in his throat. No!

Aiden looked at his suspended leg and felt a rush of pure, blinding anger.

None of this was all right.

4

It had been a very long and stressful day for Katie. Like on most mornings, she'd started off waking, showering, and getting the kids something healthy for breakfast. While Jon's restaurant, No Ka 'Oi, didn't technically open until eleven a.m., her husband's duties as managing chef required him to start work hours earlier, leaving her solo for morning duty at home. Not that she minded. She was incredibly proud of the restaurant. In fact, it was her idea to market it as a pure farm-to-market establishment and for Jon to oversee acquiring the food he served on a menu that changed daily.

Every day, their fishermen went out in small boats to catch a variety of fish—tropical Ono, mahi-mahi and bottom fish like Opakapaka, Onaga, lei, and Uku, caught at depths of two thousand feet and slowly brought to the surface; fighting Ahi caught far out at sea with fast boats trolling lures; papio from the lagoons near the shores north of Pa'ia; and moi from fish ponds on their family's land. The fish were brought directly to Jon every morning. He processed and served it within twenty-four hours with the name of the fishman listed in the menu he printed before opening each morning. Jon's restaurant was also known for its specialty sauces, recipes made from Hana limes and coconut milk, mangoes and macadamia nuts grown right on the grounds of Pali Maui. Lobster and coconut soup might be followed with a Haiku tomato and Maui onion salad drizzled with a Tahitian vanilla dressing.

Jon's attention to detail garnered attention from critics. No Ka 'Oi was featured in many prestigious travel magazines, including *Conde Nast*.

The upside was that Katie's gift shop and plantation tours were located only a short distance away, both on Pali Maui, their family's pineapple plantation. This allowed her to see her husband throughout the day, even if he was too busy to chat, as was often the case.

Christel also worked at Pali Maui. As a lawyer, she oversaw all the legal, financial, and general business aspects of the business. Their mother directed the farming operation, with the help of Miguel Nakamoa, their faithful farm manager, who had been with their mother since the inception of Pali Maui.

The entire family was extremely busy. Yet when word came of Aiden's accident, they all dropped everything and raced to the hospital.

The hours of waiting had been grueling. She hadn't realized how sitting and drinking stale coffee could sap your strength. Of course, anxiety played into the equation and was likely the culprit for her feeling like she'd just swam two hundred yards against incoming waves on Jaws Beach, the most powerful—and often dangerous—surfing beaches on the island.

Katie glanced in her rearview mirror. Noelle slept soundly in her car seat. It would be a shame to wake her. The real trick would be to getting her back down if she woke. And Katie was far too tired to deal with a fussy toddler screaming to play with Givey, their Cavapoo puppy.

She gripped the steering wheel a little tighter and

squelched a yawn as she followed Jon's car into the neighborhood. When they turned onto their street, Katie immediately noticed a large moving truck in front of the house next door. The property had been vacant for over four months after the family living there moved back to the mainland.

She'd always meant to get to know the wife. Sadly, she'd been too busy, especially with her failed merchandising endeavor with Latham Enterprises. She's spent hours secretly putting together that deal only to learn she would never go into business with Greer Latham. If she ever saw that louse again, it would be far too soon for her liking.

Suddenly, Jon's brake lights came on. Katie slammed her foot onto her own brakes to keep from rear-ending her husband's car.

As soon as they both came to a full stop, Katie flung open her door and jumped out. "Jon, what in world are you doing? I could've slammed into you. Never mind the jolt might have woke Noelle." She didn't mean to be so accusatory, but the day's events had worn her thin.

Jon quickly apologized. He pointed to their driveway, which was filled with boxes and furniture—a worn floral-print sofa and what looked to be an oak dining table and chairs. A rolled-up rug laid across the strip of lawn between the two properties.

"What is going on?" she asked. "Why is our driveway blocked?"

Jon shrugged. "I'm not sure. But I'll find out."

Her husband headed in the direction of the moving truck. Before he'd made a half dozen paces, a man appeared. He looked to be in his sixties, wore baggy pants and a T-shirt that said "Oh, I'm sorry. I forgot I only exist when you need something." The snarl on the man's face matched his mean-spirited T-shirt. Worse, his bare stomach poked out between that shirt and his belt.

"Hey," the man said. "Move your vehicles. I'm paying these

schmucks a hundred bucks an hour and I don't need any delays in the process."

Katie could see Jon take a deep breath. "Uh, yeah. I understand. Unfortunately, we live here." He pointed to their house. "And we can't park in our driveway."

"Well, you're just going to have to move those cars on down the street a bit," the guy replied, not budging an inch on his earlier request.

Jon looked shocked. Still, he shrugged his shoulders. "Yeah, okay. Well, do you know when this stuff will be cleared out of our driveway?"

Katie's shoulders automatically tightened. *There goes Jon*, she thought. *Always standing down in a confrontation. Never making a scene.*

"Sir," she said, stepping forward. "We're sympathetic to your situation. However, we've been at the hospital all day and have a sleeping child in the car. We're tired and need to get to bed. We're going to have to ask you to move your belongings so we can get in our driveway."

Did they have to park in the driveway right now? Perhaps not. But it was the principle of the thing. If this grouch of a guy thought he was going to step onto her property and issue her orders, he was severely mistaken.

She met the man's gaze and never looked away. She'd read in a book that this tactic was essential for women who wanted to be empowered and successful—both in business and in these types of situations. *If you're going to try to intimidate me*, she thought. *You had better be ready for some serious push-back.*

Jon put his arm around her shoulders in a silent message. "Sir, I don't think we got your name. We're going to be neighbors, so we should get to know each other." He reached out his hand. "I'm Jon Ackerman. This is my wife, Katie. We have two daughters. Willa is fifteen and Noelle is not yet two. Oh, and we have a dog. Givey." He paused. "But rest assured, he doesn't bark."

The man stood with his arms crossed and remained silent.

"And your name?" Jon prompted.

"Spud Weaver. Legal name Cecil." He tilted his head in the direction of the moving truck. "Afraid that stuff is going to remain where it's at." He glared at Katie. "At least until morning."

"I could help you move your things, if that's the issue," Jon offered.

"It's staying 'til morning," the grouchy man repeated.

Katie felt a stab of anger so swift and sudden, it surprised her. Her nerves were already stretched to the breaking point. Who did this guy think he was? Maybe she'd just turn on her sprinklers and soak his things. That would show him!

Better yet, she'd call the police.

Knowing what she was likely thinking, her husband tightened his grip around her shoulders. "Okay. Well, we'll just park down the street. For this one night. Uh, welcome to the neighborhood."

Before Katie could protest, he pulled her away. As they walked in the direction of their cars, she couldn't hold in her frustration any longer. "Why did you do that? He has no right to put his crap furniture in our driveway. I mean, what kind of person does that?"

Jon ran his hand through the top of his hair. "Look, Katie. We'll sort it out tomorrow. Until then, let's get Noelle out of the car and into bed." He glanced up at the second-floor window that was lit up. "And we need to check on Willa. Make sure she's had dinner and that she did her homework."

"But—"

"Please, Katie," he pleaded.

She let him guide her to her car, but not before she looked over her shoulder.

Spud-whatever-his-name was still stood looking at them with his arms crossed. *Yeah, welcome to the neighborhood,* she thought. But inside, she was pulling the welcome mat out from under that awful man's feet.

5

The following morning, they all gathered at the hospital again. Aiden's second surgery, the one to correct his ankle, was scheduled for early afternoon and his family wanted to be there. Christel was the first to arrive and was surprised to find her mother asleep in the waiting room with multiple empty Styrofoam cups on the floor next to her.

Her mother's eyes opened when Christel bent to gather the coffee cups. "Oh, honey," she said, rubbing at her eyes. She sat up and glanced at her watch. "What time is it?"

"Mom, have you been here all night?" Christel asked.

"No, I went home and got something to eat. Something healthy. I thought I could go to bed and get rest. Unfortunately, I couldn't quit thinking about Aiden here alone. I know he's a grown man and I'm being silly, but..."

Christel patted her hand. "You don't have to explain."

Christel wasn't surprised to learn her mother had returned after only a few hours. One thing was indisputable. Ava Briscoe would always be there for her children, and sometimes even when she wasn't necessarily needed. Christel and her siblings knew they came first, no matter what.

When Christel's marriage began to falter, it was her mother who spent countless hours holding her hand and listening. That was one of her best qualities. Her mother didn't offer uninvited advice or urge her to take steps she wasn't ready for. She was simply there. Her strength had become Christel's strength. Frankly, she wasn't entirely sure she would have gotten through that heartbreaking divorce without her mother by her side.

In the months following her split with Jay, she'd often reached for the phone and began dialing his number, convinced she'd made a mistake. She could barely remember a time when she didn't love Jay Bruening or the way his dimples deepened when he smiled at her. In the end, none of that mattered. If she had remained Jay's wife, his addiction would have destroyed her.

Jay's rapid decline and the end of her marriage felt humiliating. How could someone who was smart and educated find herself in that situation? Likely because she'd only wanted to see the best in him, not his worst. It crushed her to discover her love wasn't enough to help him battle and beat the demons inside.

Her mother had assured her she was doing the right thing. That was over two years ago, and she still doubted her decision to break it off. More than that, she missed Jay and still worried about him. No divorce decree could control her heart.

Christel watched as her mother pulled a comb and mirror from her purse.

Now it was her turn to be there for her mom, a new widow who had been bulldozed with grief followed by her own shocking discovery.

"Mom." She placed her hand on her mother's arm. "Are you hungry? Can I go get you some breakfast?"

Before her mother could answer, the elevator doors opened, and Katie entered the waiting room. "Morning. I'm alone today," she announced. "Jon agreed to get the girls where they needed to be. How's Aiden?"

Their mother reported that Aiden had a fitful night. The nurses had to increase his pain meds. "He's been through a lot," she said. "I'll just be glad to get these surgeries behind us and get him home with me."

"Did you spend the night here?" Katie asked. "No offense, but your clothes are rumpled and your mascara has seen better days."

Christel gave her a look.

"What? I'm just saying," Katie said, defending herself.

"I was just going down to get Mom some breakfast. Why don't you come with me to help carry everything up?" Christel pulled on her sister's arm, not leaving much room for her to say no.

"Okay, yeah. We'll be right back, Mom." Katie followed Christel out of the waiting room and down a long hallway lined with framed photos of men and women in business attire who were on the hospital board. "What's the matter, Christel? Did you wake up in a mood?"

"No, I did not wake up in a mood. I simply thought pointing out how bad Mom looked wasn't in her best interests this morning. Especially after a night on that hard sofa."

Katie nodded. "She slept here? How awful, but I'm not entirely surprised. Yeah, I suppose I didn't need to point out how rugged she looked. I didn't mean anything by it."

That's the way she and Katie were. They were frank with each other, spoke their minds even if what they had to say might not land well. Neither of them was prone to take offense. Any hurt feelings were quickly mended. They were sisters. They loved each other.

Katie hoisted her purse strap up a little higher on her

shoulder. "Boy, wait until you hear what happened to us last night." She told Christel all about the new neighbor, about how grouchy he was and how out of line he had been placing his possessions on their property and refusing to move them, even when Jon asked nicely. She even told her about her plan to baptize his belongings with her hose.

Christel raised her eyebrows. "No. You didn't really douse his stuff with the sprinkler?"

Katie sighed. "No. It seemed juvenile. But I wanted to." She nodded as they passed some nurses in the hallway. "I think he's going to be trouble," Katie remarked.

"He actually left his furniture in your driveway all night?"

"Yes. It was still there when I left this morning even though the moving truck was gone. It took everything in me not to march over and pound on his door. Nothing would have given me more pleasure than waking his grouchy fanny."

That made Christel laugh. "Well, why didn't you?"

"Because I promised Jon I'd try and be nice. He thinks nothing will be gained from being enemies with our next-door neighbor. Truthfully, I think we're already there," she confided. "That guy is strange, and a little bit mean." Katie told him about the T-shirt saying and how he'd folded his arms and glared at them.

"Well, legally you were in the right," Christel told her. "City ordinances would likely support you calling the Salvation Army to haul everything off. If he fails to move that stuff," she added.

"I know. It didn't matter. I don't think this guy is accustomed to complying with rules and regulations, even if breaking them might land him in court."

Christel huffed. "He may think differently if he has to pull out his wallet. When a judge orders him to pay damages, he might change his tune. In this case, that would be the cost of removing his items from your property."

Katie shrugged. "You're assuming my nice husband would ever agree to sue someone, let alone a neighbor."

The hospital cafeteria was packed. People dressed in scrubs lined up in front of a glass sneeze-guarded buffet and waited their turn for the cafeteria attendant to scoop scrambled eggs and bacon onto their plates.

Christel pointed to an overhead sign announcing the breakfast special was French toast topped with fresh berries. "Mom would like that, don't you think?"

When they'd finished paying at the check-out counter, Christel and Katie made their way back to the waiting room. The surgeon was there speaking with their mother.

"We plan to operate at one," he told her. "The procedure will be fairly straightforward. We'll be performing a lateral ankle ligament reconstruction, also known as the Bostrom procedure."

Their mother frowned. "What does that entail?"

He gave her a reassuring smile. "I promise you, after what Aiden faced yesterday, this is nothing. Often, this procedure is done on an outpatient basis. We'll simply go in and repair those torn ligaments and be done."

Christel felt her face flush. Even more so when he turned and looked at her. His lips drew into a smile. "Good morning. I was just telling your mom about the day's plan regarding your brother."

Katie placed her food laden tray on the table next to the sofa. "Our family is so appreciative of everything you and the hospital staff are doing to take care of Aiden."

Christel tried to think of what to say, how to say it. "I—yes, thank you," she finally forced out. She remembered yesterday and how she'd flung herself into his arms. The thought now embarrassed her to the point she could not meet his gaze. Instead, she stared at his name tag. "Evan Matisse, M.D."

Her mom's voice pulled her attention. "Christel?"

She looked up and realized she hadn't been listening. "I'm sorry. What?"

"Dr. Matisse asked if you had any questions," Katie offered, giving her a look.

"I'm sorry. No questions. I think we all understand what is ahead." *Well, that sounded a little lame.*

It took her a few seconds to collect herself and force a pathetic smile. While she would never admit the fact out loud, Dr. Matisse made her flustered. It was his eyes. He almost looked dangerous—until he smiled.

A surge of loneliness suddenly came over her, settling deep and heavy in her heart. She missed so much. The empty spot in her bed left her feeling untethered. She missed having strong arms reach for her in the middle of the night. Missed waking to a man's urgent touch, feeling his body against her own. Even more, she missed having a partner. Simple everyday things like having someone to chat about the weather with, someone to watch television with. Someone to argue with about taking out the trash and replacing the lid on the peanut butter...someone by her side as she journeyed through life. Sure, she had her family. It wasn't the same.

She let her eyes drift back to Dr. Matisse. He studied her for a moment, those eyes narrowing as if to seek out the place where she couldn't hide from him. She didn't know whether to blush or be annoyed.

He turned his attention to her mom, assuring her that he would check back in after the surgery with a report. He placed his hand on her mother's arm. "Don't worry," he said. "I will take care of your son as if he were my own."

Dr. Matisse turned to leave. Before he did, he glanced her way and smiled.

As soon as he was out of hearing range, Katie poked her elbow into Christel's side. "He's gorgeous. And I think he likes you."

"Don't be ridiculous," Christel countered. "And stop with the matchmaking already." She launched into another severe reprimand for not taking her profile down from the dating site. "I don't enjoy warding off the advances of guys like Web Green."

Katie's eyebrows lifted. "Web Green? Now that's a name from the past."

Christel explained what had happened when she got pulled over for driving too fast, and how Web had urged her to go out with him, mentioning the dating site.

Their mom reached for the container of food. "You were cited for speeding?"

"Not exactly," Christel admitted. "Seems he still has a crush on me." She directed her attention back at her sister. "I hope I made myself clear. I want that down."

"You don't have to get so testy," Katie told her with a slight laugh. "I was only trying to help. Besides, looks like my efforts may have saved you from having to pay a fine."

"Well, that's debatable. Regardless, I don't need your help in that department." Christel raised her chin. "I don't need your matchmaking skills, thank you."

Christel stated her position firmly. Yet, in the back of her mind, she couldn't help but ponder her sister's earlier claim about the doctor liking her...and she smiled.

6

Aiden lay in the hospital bed and stared at the ceiling. It'd been a week since the accident. The first few days were rough. The pain was pretty outrageous. Thankfully, the hospital staff had been generous with the pain meds.

On day three, they'd moved him out of the critical care unit. While he was still uncomfortable and had pain, his injuries continued to improve. Already he was feeling anxious to get out of this place. Despite the constant visits from his family, he was going out of his mind with boredom. He'd even counted the ceiling tiles. As far as he could tell, there were thirty-two—one with a slight stain.

The isolation in between visitors was killing him. Unfortunately, he'd lost his cell phone in the explosion. His mother promised she was working on getting it replaced. So, there was that. At least then he could browse social media. In the meantime, he had no choice but to entertain himself with network television. Like most hospitals, there was no Netflix or any other subscriber channels. Even cable was limited to primarily news.

And don't even get him started on the hospital food. A guy

could consume only so many dried-out pork chops and frozen peas before his stomach rebelled. Maybe his brother-in-law would take pity and send Katie to sneak in food that was more palatable.

The door opened and a tall, gray-haired man in a white coat sauntered in. The door squeaked shut behind him. "Hi, I'm Dr. Egan."

The new visitor sat down and scooted his plastic chair close to the bed. "Dr. Matisse was up all night performing an emergency surgery. I'm covering so he can catch some sleep." He buried his attention on a clipboard where he flipped through paperwork. "Well, young man. Looks like you're progressing nicely."

Aiden straightened in the bed the best he could given his leg still swung from a metal bar. "What's the plan? When do you think I'll get to ditch this contraption and get out of here?" He pointed to the metal bar suspended above the bed.

Dr. Egan smiled. "Well, that's a good sign. When patients start begging to go home, we count that as a signal they are healing." He gave Aiden a sympathetic look. "I know you must be anxious, son. But trust me, you want to give that leg plenty of time to heal properly. Dr. Matisse is a highly regarded orthopedic specialist and has developed your treatment plan. I'm sure he'll go over those plans with you and answer all your questions. If it's any consolation, traction isn't used as often, or for as long, as in the past." He nodded in the direction of the bar. "That should be a short-term thing. Even so, these things take time. Like I said, you don't want to be up and around too early."

That was not what Aiden wanted to hear. More time in this hospital bed wasn't something he embraced with any sense of anticipation. He needed his life back. He was in the middle of renovating his house and he needed to return to work. The sooner he could start rehab, the better.

In addition to his primary duties at Maui Emergency Management, he served as the liaison between his agency and MSAR, the volunteer search and rescue team here on the island. He'd worked hard to foster cooperation between the two units but there was always a slight competition between the two agencies and a few personalities that tended to clash. It was essential that he get back as soon as possible.

Dr. Egan stood. "What I can promise is that the nurses will continue to take good care of you. Don't be hesitant to push that call button any time you need something." His face broke into an encouraging smile. "You'll be out of here and good as new very soon." He patted the bedcovers, then turned and left the room, leaving Aiden to go back to staring at the ceiling tiles.

Minutes later, the door opened again. This time, his boss peeked his head in. "So, hey...you up for some visitors?"

Aiden enthusiastically nodded. "You bet."

Captain Dennis inched through the door, followed by Grant Costa and Jeremy Hogan. "Hey, man," Jeremy said. "Good to see you."

Grant nodded. "Scary deal. I don't mind saying...we were worried we'd lost you."

Captain Dennis bobbed his head in agreement. "Yeah, that little incident scraped about ten years off my life."

"Really?" Jeremy bumped Captain Dennis' shoulder. "Didn't stop you from putting in bids for his stuff. Right, Grant?"

Grant shrugged. "I mean, if you were dead, I wouldn't sell your stuff right away. I'd wait a few days out of respect. But it never hurts to take bids."

Aiden laughed. "Great. Glad to know you guys care so deeply."

They all knew the work they did was dangerous at times, but the reality of what that truly meant had hit home for all of them, and especially for Aiden. Sometimes humor was a fail-safe. And sometimes it was okay to be vulnerable. "I'm pretty darned glad to be here," he told them, his throat catching on the last word.

"Hey, there he is."

Aiden looked past the guys to see Megan McCord entering the room. She held a silly bunch of colored helium balloons. "For you," she said, tying them to the end of the bed.

Aiden groaned. "Balloons?"

Jeremy laughed. "What's the matter, Aiden? Don't you like balloons?"

Megan parked her hands on her petite hips. "Everybody likes balloons. Unless they think it'll hurt their tough image." She had a smile on her face, but her tone was clearly a challenge.

He tried not to frown. Why did it always feel like this woman was pushing at him?

Aiden shook off his irritation. "Pretty hard to feel tough with your leg suspended from a bar."

And what was it with that tiger tattoo laced up her arm? He had nothing against tattoos, but the females he knew chose a rose or a few sentimental words. What kind of woman would permanently decorate her skin with a snarling animal? Someone who was trying too hard to be a badass, that's who.

Megan almost smiled, then placed her hand on Captain Dennis's shoulder. "Well, I hope you know everything's being taken care of, so don't you worry a bit."

The captain nodded. "Yeah, Megan here has really stepped up. She offered to cover for you. So, you just take all the time you need to get well, Aiden. No worries."

The guys all rallied around the bed. "Yeah, what he said. She's got everything handled."

Megan lifted her chin slightly. "I worked with volunteer teams in Oregon. There's definitely an art to motivating people who are offering their time as opposed to the ones getting a paycheck. Everyone responds to a job well done. The key is to provide essential training and lather on the praise at every opportunity."

Irritation tightened Aiden's muscles. He fisted and released his hands. The last thing he needed was for Megan McCord to horn in on his duties. There was something about her he just didn't like. Her arrogance, for starts. Not only did she go above and beyond to prove she was just like one of the guys, she seemed to think she was better and more skilled than most. Sure, she was beautiful. Angelina Jolie gorgeous. But she made sure everyone knew it.

That attitude and all that self-promotion would get someone hurt. Would she have risked returning for a final look to make sure everyone was off that boat? Would she have taken the hit he had? Doubt it.

Truth was...he didn't entirely trust her.

A nurse entered and quietly moved to his side. Wordlessly, she checked the blinking monitors and made a note in his chart.

"Well, hey," Captain Dennis said. "We shouldn't stay long. Just wanted to drop by and check on you."

Jeremy ran a hand through the top of his hair. "Yeah, if you need anything, just reach out."

Megan echoed the same. "Yeah, just give a holler."

An uncomfortable silence fell between them. Captain Dennis finally spoke up. "We'll check back in with you soon."

Minutes later, they were gone.

Aiden was left to ponder the fact he'd been replaced at work, even if temporarily. The idea didn't set well with him. Not at all.

He let out a defeated sigh, looked up, and went back to counting the ceiling tiles.

7

Ava shook the crisp sheets over the guest bed and tucked in the sides. It had been three weeks since her son's unfortunate accident, and Dr. Matisse had finally given the go ahead for Aiden's release from the hospital.

Dr. Matisse had cautioned that a fractured femur takes the longest of any bone in the body to heal. Not only that, breaking a femur could make everyday tasks much more difficult to maneuver. In the explosion, Aiden had been thrown against the side of the boat, resulting in two fractures of his right femur. Likely, the extensive injury could double the amount of time necessary for the leg to fully heal.

Knowing how hard it was going to be for her son not to be able to return directly to his own place, she wanted everything here at her house as comfortable as possible which was why she was putting him in the guest room that had garden doors leading out to the pool. He could open them and catch the breeze at night.

Aiden had made remarkable progress. From early on, her son was determined to push hard for improvement. Though at times, she suspected he wasn't entirely honest about his level of pain. He was like his father in that he didn't like feeling vulnerable.

A sudden twinge of painful sadness crept into Ava's heart. She briefly paused her duties and placed an open hand to her chest. She hadn't thought about Lincoln for days, maybe even a week. Which was surprising actually, given the mental intrusion she fought daily in those early days right after the accident that took his life and the horrible weeks that followed. No matter what she promised herself, thoughts of her late husband and all the *why* questions continued to bombard her waking moments.

She'd be in the office with Christel going over revenue and expense figures and she could swear she heard Lincoln's voice outside. She'd be in the packing shed with Mig reviewing inspection reports and she'd think she spotted him over at the conveyor belt. He always had a thing for checking to make sure the conveyors were properly working and that the pineapples were getting sufficiently waxed for transport.

In the mornings, she'd pull out the carton of eggs from the refrigerator and crack four before remembering she only needed two now. The worst was when she wasn't quite awake and she'd reach for him in bed and he wasn't there.

Of course, her husband hadn't been fully present for a long while prior to his passing. The fact he'd been with someone else left her feeling weightless and heavy, all at the same time.

She wondered why she hadn't sensed it. Why hadn't she known he no longer belonged to her? And what had prompted him to leave her for the arms of another woman who was barely grown...the daughter of her best friend?

She would never have answers to those questions and, in many ways, she'd wrapped her head around that. Still, she'd been married to Lincoln Briscoe for a long time, decades even. You couldn't simply erase that in a day and turn off all your feelings, even if you had decided to move on.

That must have been what Christel felt early after her painful separation from Jay. As her mother, she'd tried her best to be there and help her daughter through the divorce—the loss of the man she'd loved.

But this? She hadn't known it felt like this.

It was true. Some kinds of pain you can't escape. You simply must move through the pain and come out the other side, somehow recapturing your joy.

It now seemed everyone she knew had a stake in helping her do just that.

A lady in Lahaina taught people how to make handcrafted bracelets using dried native island flowers encased in resin. Katie had signed her up for classes. Ava wasn't very good at it and by the third lesson, she begged off. "I appreciate the gesture, Katie. It just isn't me."

Christel thought it would be good for Ava to join her for an advanced investment course digitally broadcast over Zoom. Unfortunately, while she found the topic interesting, she couldn't seem to keep her mind from drifting. She'd read grief was like that. Having trouble focusing was common.

Shane's big idea was to show up on Sunday afternoons for dinner. Granted, he'd often done that before Lincoln died, but she appreciated having someone to talk to besides employees, investors and customers. Plus, she learned new things. Like the fact Shane had ended his relationship with Aimee Battista, a girl he'd met first at dinner with his brothers and sisters and then again at Black Rock.

At first, it appeared her youngest had fallen for this girl. In the early part of their relationship, they were nearly inseparable. Shane had taken the loss of his father and what he'd done especially hard. The cute little blonde seemed the perfect diversion. So, Ava was surprised to learn the two of them had decided to put the brakes on their close friendship. "Everything was beginning to get a little too heavy," he explained. "I'm not ready for a long-term commitment or anything."

That was an understatement. She still thought of her youngest as her baby. She'd coddled him a bit too much, or at least Lincoln had thought so. The result was a young man who seemed to have little direction and next to no desire to be productive. He much preferred days filled with fun.

Ava was hoping he was finally maturing a bit. It certainly appeared he was making movement in that direction with this new girl. It was the first time he'd dated someone for more than a week. Sadly, the relationship had ended.

Apparently, Aimee wanted a career in entertainment and had moved to Los Angeles to find her fame. Frankly, you couldn't find two young people better matched than Shane and Aimee. Neither of them had any real sense of what it meant to be a responsible adult. Ava took heart believing Shane would eventually mature, settle down, and get serious. Her other children had. She wasn't really worried. Her youngest son would as well.

Strangely, Aiden hadn't come around all that much. Oh, he'd show up for family night or anytime the Briscoes gathered for a special dinner out. But she sensed a distance in her oldest that hadn't been there before, like his struggle was more than he could wrestle.

He'd buried himself in work spending long days at the station and volunteered to go on every call he could. It almost seemed as if he invited danger and needed the adrenaline rush he said his job often provided. That attitude likely contributed to his getting hurt in the explosion. His boss had confided he'd had a bit of trouble getting Aiden to exit the boat, even when assured all the passengers were safely off.

Ava ran her hands over the pillowcase and let out a heavy sigh. Hopefully, she'd get to the bottom of what was up with him while he was here recuperating. They'd have lots of time together.

That is, if her best friend Alani didn't sign her up for another gardening class.

CHRISTEL WAITED IMPATIENTLY for the garage door to open while holding three big plastic bags of trash in her hands. For a single woman, she created an unbelievable amount of refuse. Perhaps it was all the frozen dinner trays, or the cartons of milk gone bad because she simply couldn't drink it fast enough.

The door reached the garage ceiling and clicked, signaling it was safe to exit. Christel juggled the weight of the bags and wandered out to the curb where she'd place the trash for pickup later that morning.

That was another thing she missed...having a husband to take out the garbage. She had just placed the bags at the curb when she heard a voice call out.

"Yoo hoo! Christel, dear!"

Christel immediately groaned. It was her chatty neighbor, Maggie. Today, she wore a brightly colored pair of cropped jeans in a floral print with a wide-brimmed hat in a matching pattern. In her gloved hands, she held a small metal hand trowel.

"I was hoping I'd catch you outside today. I mentioned earlier that I'm cooking dinner on Friday night and I'm hoping you might reconsider and join us."

"Us?"

Maggie grinned. "I've invited my new doctor friend. I'd love for you to meet him."

Christel's mind raced. She didn't want to hurt the old woman's feelings. No doubt Maggie meant well, but her matchmaking was annoying. The last thing she needed was to have to make conversation with some ill-suited guy.

"Uh, I don't think so, Maggie. I promised my mother I'd do something with her."

"Oh, I understand." Her neighbor shook her head. "When my Harry died, it took a long time to adjust." Her face broke into an understand smile. "Maybe another time."

Christel nodded. "Oh, yes. Another time." She let out a sigh of relief and waved to Maggie before heading back inside, determined to remember to glance outside the window for any sign of her neighbor before ever leaving the house again.

But on Friday, she got home from work early and donned her most comfortable robe, the ratty one Jay used to tease her about saying it looked like the skin of a dead wooly animal. She didn't care. She loved the way the soft worn fabric felt against her skin after her bath.

After opening the refrigerator and finding little inside that interested her, she moved to the pantry and pulled a bag of microwave popcorn from its package. Not exactly nutritious but who would know? There was an upside to being single, she supposed. She never had to answer for any of her food choices.

She had just pulled the freshly popped corn from the microwave and was pouring it into a bowl when she heard laughter. She moved to the sink and peeked out the window, surprised to see a guy walking up Maggie's sidewalk.

That's right. Her neighbor's dinner party was planned for tonight.

A woman's laughter rang out, which caused Christel to stretch for a better view. Yes, she'd become one of those neighbors—the ones who couldn't seem to mind their own business.

As the couple drew closer, her brows pulled into a deep frown. The man—Maggie's doctor friend—was Dr. Matisse!

And he was laughing and talking with an attractive woman. She wore fitted jeans, a white silky blouse, and a stylish pair of drop earrings that peeked nicely out from her long dark hair. Dr. Matisse wore a pair of light-colored chinos and a navy dinner jacket over top of a white button-down shirt.

The laughing couple reached the front door and Dr. Matisse reached for the doorbell. His other hand went to the woman's back as Maggie opened her door and bid them inside.

A twinge of unexpected jealousy caused her stomach to pull in on itself.

She huffed. *That* was the doctor her neighbor wanted to hook her up with?

Her shoulders drooped as she marched to her trash basket and tossed the popcorn inside. It seemed she suddenly no longer had an appetite.

8

Katie closed the dishwasher door and wiped her hands on a towel. "Willa!" she hollered. "Hurry up. We're running late."

"Geez, Mom. I can hear. You don't have to yell," Willa said as she made her way down the stairs. She grabbed her backpack from the hook by the door and slung it onto her shoulder. "And I need twenty dollars."

"I gave you money yesterday, Willa. Where'd that go?" Katie grabbed the rag from the sink and wiped the counter down.

"Uh...let's see. I had to pay for my volleyball uniform and lunch."

Katie's eyes widened with suspicion. "That blew through fifty bucks?"

Willa rolled her eyes. "Okay, I spent a little."

"More than a little, it sounds like." Katie ran the rag under the running faucet. "Tell you what, you take the garbage out and I'll give you ten. And that's a lot for a single chore. Tonight, when your father gets home, we'll talk about how you can earn more. Your parents aren't a money tree, you know."

"I already watch Noelle all the time," Willa complained. "No one else at school has to watch their little sister and do chores."

Katie folded the rag and placed it in over the sink divider. "I doubt that." She turned and faced her daughter. "Look, we don't have time to argue about this right now. You're fifteen and it's time you take on some more responsibility. Perhaps we can even find some summer work for you at Pali Maui. Until then, you'll just have to endure some household chores." She pointed at the overflowing garbage can she'd pulled out from under the sink. "That, for starters."

Willa groaned. "Dad would've given me the money without all these strings attached." She lifted the full garbage bag from the trash container and made a face. "Ew...it smells."

No doubt, Katie thought as she pulled Noelle from her highchair. "C'mon, sweetheart. Let's get you cleaned up."

A couple of minutes later, Willa returned still carrying the garbage bag. "Hey, Mom...there's no room in the trash bin. So what do you want me to do with this?" She held up the bag, still wincing at the smell.

Katie frowned. "That can't be. Trash pick-up was just yesterday. No one has taken any trash out. Here...hold your sister." She handed off Noelle and headed out to check the situation.

Sure enough. The bin was filled. In fact, it was overfilled and threatened to spill out. From the scattered coffee-stained envelopes at her feet, it appeared some of it already had.

Katie bent and carefully picked up one of the envelopes by grasping a clean corner. She held it up so she could get a better look. Upon examination, she huffed.

The nerve of that man!

She turned and marched back inside, picked up her phone off the counter and dialed Jon.

"What's the matter, Mom?" Willa asked.

Katie didn't answer. She simply held up a finger in a signal that she would answer after the call.

Jon picked up on the third ring. "Hi, babe. What's up?"

Katie tightened her grip on the phone. "What's up? I'll tell you what's up. That nasty man—Spud Whatever—well, he helped himself to our garbage receptacle. Filled it to the brim with his trash. That guy has a lot of moxie if he thinks we're going to put up with that!"

"Honey, calm down," Jon said. "I'll pay our new neighbor a visit and handle the situation when I get home. It could be that he—"

"Don't you dare make excuses for that awful man," she scolded. "I knew he was going to be trouble." She started to say more but was interrupted by a loud clatter in the background on Jon's end. "What's that?" she asked her husband.

"Uh, just a little mishap in the kitchen. Look, honey…I've got to go. I'll look into this tonight. Love you." He hung up.

Katie pulled the phone from her ear and stared at it. He didn't really just hang up on her? Worse, she knew exactly how her husband would take care of the situation. He'd go over and be all nice and end up letting their neighbor off the hook.

Well, that was *not* going to happen.

She glanced at the wall clock and let out a huff. Some things were worth being late for.

"Stay with your sister," she barked at Willa as she headed for the front door.

"Mom, we're going to be late. Where are you going?"

"Stay with your sister," Katie repeated. "This won't take long."

Minutes later, she was standing on Spud Weaver's doorstep. She drew her hand into a fist and banged on the painted wood.

Nothing.

She pulled herself a little straighter and gave it another go… banged a little harder.

Nothing.

She went to bang a third time when the door opened. There stood their new neighbor wearing a badly stained T-shirt...and boxer shorts.

The sight caused her to stammer. "Oh, I—"

Katie couldn't finish her sentence before her neighbor cut her off. "What d'ya want?" he growled. "Don't you know it's early? Can't a man sleep in?" He peered out and glanced up and down their street. "Nothing seems to be on fire. So, what is it?" He glared.

Not to be deterred, Katie lifted her chin and glared back. "You put your trash in our garbage receptacle." She pointed in the direction of the alley. "It's full."

"Yeah...so." He rubbed his belly and yawned.

"It's *our* trash bin." She cleared her throat. "That's rude... and unacceptable."

He laughed. "Oh, it is...is it?"

Now it was Katie's turn to growl. She jabbed her finger in his direction. "Let me make something very clear. You may think it's just fine to disrespect other people's property, but make no mistake...you're bucking with the wrong neighbors. We won't stand for it."

"That alleyway is public property, is it not?"

"Yes, but—"

"And your trash bin was on public property?" He rubbed his scruffy unshaven chin. "I guess that entitles me to use it. Besides, how did I know it belonged to you? Was your name on it?"

Katie parked her hands on her hips. "Well, you are now on notice that it belongs to us. You are not to use it." She took a breath, gaining steam. "And you are not to store your belongings on our property either. Am I making myself clear?"

Spud let go of an amused chuckle. "Boy, you sure get yourself worked up over a whole lot of nothing."

Katie filled her chest with air. "Well, that's all I have to say. Except that, when you answer the door, it's polite to wear pants." She turned and marched down his sidewalk.

9

"Then I just told him we were not going to put up with his antics any longer," Katie said, reaching for a warm brownie still in the baking pan.

Ava playfully slapped at her daughter's fingers. "Can't you at least wait until I get them on a plate?" It did her heart good to see all four of her children in her kitchen again. This was a sight she'd never, ever take for granted. Not for the rest of her life.

"I call the other corner," Shane warned while leaning over the counter from where he sat on Ava's barstool, much like he had as a kid.

It was Briscoe family tradition that each of her four children got one of the corner brownies when she pulled a batch from the oven. In a family with three older siblings, Shane had learned his siblings could not always be trusted.

"So, what did your neighbor say?" Christel asked.

"Not much," Katie reported. "I think I got my point across."

"Bet the old coot didn't see that coming," Aiden said, laughing as he hobbled across the room on his crutches. He winced with pain.

"Do you need some pain meds, honey?" Ava offered. "Maybe you should sit down."

He shook his head no. "Thanks, Mom. I'm good."

Ava knew she might be over-mothering her son. She wasn't one of those helicopter moms who hovered over her children, but this was different. Or, maybe losing Lincoln had made her different.

While it had been several weeks since the accident and Dr. Matisse was pleased with Aiden's progress, Ava still worried. Her son was still having trouble sleeping. The alert on the security motion detectors Lincoln had installed in the main living area nearly always woke her as well. Early on, she got up to see if her son needed anything. This seemed to only aggravate him, so she'd stopped. She forced herself to back off and let him have his space, but that didn't mean she didn't remain concerned.

Ava went to the cupboard for some plates. Shane winked at Christel. Disregarding his mother's admonition to wait, he lifted a corner brownie. When the others all protested, he simply took a big bite. "What? Katie got hers?"

Katie took pity and grabbed one for Aiden as well who stood teetering on his crutches. He favored her with a grin. "Thanks."

Ava watched from across the kitchen. She rolled her eyes and put the stack of plates she was holding back in the cupboard then rejoined her grown children at the kitchen island.

Aiden awkwardly slid into a barstool, leaned his crutches against the counter. He took a bite of his brownie. Still chewing, he looked across the marble island top at his youngest sister. "So, let me get this straight. Your new neighbor filled your trash bin with his garbage and you marched over and gave him the what for. I bet he didn't see that coming."

Katie beamed with pride. "Nope. I happily report I think it was a bit of a Frisbee to the head."

Shane reached for a second brownie. "Funny, you don't look that evil."

Katie grinned. "Makeup helps." She gave Shane a harsh look when he went for a third brownie. "Hey, slow down and leave some for the rest of us."

Ava reached for her own brownie, smiling inside. This... these family gatherings had seen her through the months following Lincoln's passing. The people sitting in this kitchen were her joy and reason for living.

She and her grown children had always been close but even more after Lincoln left them. Sometimes they all assembled to eat dinner together, or play some rowdy and very competitive board games. Other times they attended a ball game and cheered on Aiden and Shane who played on the same city league team in Lahaina. It also wasn't unusual for them to meet out by the reefs south of Lahaina for some surfing.

Aiden's injuries had put physical activities on hold, which didn't seem to be sitting well with him. He'd been in a mood ever since getting released from the hospital. Her son seemed short-tempered and was an all-around grouch, which was so out of character. Aiden was struggling with this new situation, she could tell. He missed all of the things he used to do, and he missed his work. It broke her heart to hear him wonder out loud about how long it would be before he could surf again.

Dr. Matisse assured him that with proper rehab he'd be able to return to all his former activities eventually but warned it could take up to six months to heal fully. In the interim, there would be many follow-up appointments, X-rays to check progress, and an extended period of rehab.

She really thought highly of her son's doctor and appreciated all the wonderful care he had provided. Dr. Matisse had gone above and beyond to keep the family well-informed, especially in those early days. After Aiden's release from the hospital, Dr. Matisse had even called Aiden on the weekend to check on him. Ava hadn't known a doctor to do that in her entire lifetime.

Christel stood. "Who wants milk?"

They all said yes, nearly in unison.

Christel moved across the kitchen floor. "Katie, help me, would you? I don't have hands."

Her sister complied. "So, when's your next appointment, Aiden?"

Ava answered for him. "Tomorrow morning at ten o'clock. And I'm glad you brought this up because I have a conflict. Weeks back, I scheduled a meeting with that new corrugated cardboard manufacturer from Georgia. He's only on island for the day or I'd reschedule. Can one of you girls possibly drive Aiden for his follow-up X-rays and doctor's appointment after?"

"Sure, Mom," Katie answered as she placed glasses on the counter. "I'm sure I can clear my plate and take Aiden."

"Thanks, sis," Aiden told her. "I hate to be any trouble."

"No trouble," she assured him. "I just have to get the girls out the door and then I'll pick you up."

Christel placed the carton of milk next to the glasses. "I'll take him. I mean, you have a family to get ready each morning and all that. I don't."

Ava raised her eyebrows. "I thought you wanted to be in on this meeting?"

Christel shook her head. "No, it's fine. I can negotiate pricing later if you decide to go with this new vendor."

Slightly puzzled, Ava reached for a glass. It wasn't like Christel to skip any meeting, let alone one that had the potential to impact Pali Maui's bottom line. "Well, okay. If you think that will work."

As a mother, she'd learned years ago not to second guess her children's decisions.

10

Christel often pressed the snooze button on her alarm clock multiple times before finally pulling herself out of bed. Not this morning. In fact, she was awake long before the alarm sounded thinking about chauffeuring Aiden to his X-rays and then for his follow up visit with Dr. Matisse.

There was no particular reason for the possibility of seeing the doctor again to take up so much of her head space. Her motivation for taking Aiden this morning was clear—she wanted to lighten Katie's burden a bit.

Okay, who was she kidding?

Ever since seeing Aiden's surgeon walk up Maggie's sidewalk with that woman, she couldn't seem to get him out of her mind. Problem was, she didn't know why?

It certainly wasn't because she had any romantic interest. That boat had sailed when her relationship with Jay ended. It would be some time before she felt ready to jump in the dating waters again. Besides, she didn't even *know* Dr. Matisse. Goodness, she didn't even know his first name.

Still, thoughts of him kept invading her head at the most

inopportune times of the day—and even her dreams. It was as if she'd lost control of her own mind.

If she were honest with herself, she didn't want to live as a single woman forever. The loneliness alone precluded her from docking on that shoreline. No, at some point she would like to fall in love again. It was just that the prospect of doing so nearly terrified her.

Christel straightened her comforter, smoothing out the wrinkles on her bed. She wandered into the bathroom, then climbed into the shower, where she allowed herself to ponder the situation a bit more because, well, overthinking was what she did best. Her biggest trepidation when it came to entering another relationship centered on Jay. Could she ever love to that extent again? Broken femurs were not the only thing that took a long time to heal.

Jay had been her first—and her only—boyfriend for many years. They'd met briefly at a beach party the summer before she'd graduated from high school. He walked straight up to her, smiled, and said, "Hey, you look a little lost. Okay if I get you a beer?"

She passed on the beer, but did join him on a piece of koa wood that had drifted up on the beach. They sat and chatted for hours. He ended up asking her out, but she declined.

She'd nearly been a zombie at the time, working and studying and freaking out about whether or not she'd gain the coveted valedictorian title in their graduating class, an honor that would surely propel her when finalizing her college applications.

Christel had never been satisfied with average. She longed to be extraordinary.

She knew from the time she was a little girl she wanted a career that could impact her world. Her goals quickly included doubling course work and obtaining her undergraduate degree in business as quickly as possible. While her counselors warned few students had a true understanding of what was required at the university level, she buckled down and surprised them all, finishing a four-year degree in three, summa cum laude.

Christel hadn't stopped there. Her hard work paid off. She had her pick of law schools and chose to attend the prestigious Loyola Law School in Chicago. There, she met like-minded young women who longed to make a difference.

They invited her to join a club on campus that focused on liberal politics. She attended a campaign rally for president hopeful Hillary Clinton. Two days later, she cut her hair into a short bob and died it blonde. She began wearing pantsuits and scoured every liberal blog she could find. In addition to long study hours, she volunteered at the local election office, helping to register voters.

It was there that she ran into one of Chicago mayor's personal aides, Paul McKee. He was slim and always perfectly dressed. There was something fussy about his appearance that suggested he spent a lot of time in front of the mirror each morning. And he smiled at you with like about two hundred brilliant white teeth.

His buddy, however, was completely the opposite.

On a Saturday morning, a familiar-looking guy wearing jeans and a casual white button-down trailed Paul into the campaign office. He had brown hair tossed boyishly around his face and nearly laughed with amusement as his eyes scanned the room.

The minute he saw her he smiled. When he did, deep dimples formed. He sauntered over. "Hey, you look a little lost. Okay if I get you a beer?" he asked, looking as if he had just unilaterally won the biggest campaign of all.

At that moment, it was as if the wind changed direction. Unfortunately, she'd discovered you can't direct the wind. You can only adjust your sails.

When Christel finished showering, she blew her hair dry. She applied makeup, taking care to draw her eyeliner with precision, then spritzed on one of her favorite colognes, generously pushing the nozzle twice for good measure.

By the time she pulled her car into the parking lot of the medical practice that housed Dr. Matisse's office, her heart was strangely pounding.

"Well, I guess we're here," she told Aiden as she craned her neck to get a better look at the premises. Nice offices with lots of windows overlooking gorgeous landscaping.

She rounded the car and pulled the passenger door open. "You need any help?" she asked her brother.

"Nah, I got it," he answered while concentrating on the best way to exit her car. She wished he would concede that he might need assistance occasionally, but he was being extremely stubborn these days.

She watched with patience as he pulled himself out of her car and positioned his crutches. Together, they made their way to the entrance.

Inside, the lobby was just as impressive. There was even a faux waterfall against the wall to the right of the front receptionist counter, giving the inside an outdoor feel.

After crossing the lobby, Aiden insisted on pushing the elevator button. "Got it," he said when she reached for it.

It dawned on her that her independent brother might ask her to remain in the waiting room while he went in to talk with his doctor. It was disturbing how disjointed the notion made her feel, like someone had pulled something she was looking forward to out from under her feet. Disappointment quickly followed.

It was then she had to admit to herself once again that by offering to drive her brother today she might not be solely trying to help out and was forced to concede she may be looking forward to seeing Dr. Matisse again. It was as if she had developed some sort of high-school crush—you know, the kind where you secretly think about a guy—a guy you barely know, but hoped to. She was...interested in Dr. Matisse.

The idea was so foreign she forgot to breathe.

She remembered how she'd felt the other night seeing him take that other woman's elbow to guide her up the steps to Maggie's front door. She'd been jealous. Admitting that now was like stepping on the scales after a weekend of binge-eating ice cream. The gain was a fact and all a person could do was lament the issue and work to remove the added weight as quickly as possible.

She simply had no business thinking that way. Not given her need for stability and peace.

Yet, it was as if her thoughts had a mind of their own.

Unlike Jay, Dr. Matisse had a rugged look about him. In fact, he resembled George Clooney. Even his black hair was peppered with gray, especially at the temples. Same went for his short-cropped beard and mustache. He was extremely tanned, like someone who spent a lot of time outdoors.

She had noticed a braided leather band occupied the spot on his right wrist where he wore his watch along with a couple of beaded wrist bracelets. Normally, she wasn't fond of men's jewelry, but the look was good on him.

While Dr. Matisse's white coat hid much of his physique, Christel could tell he was fit. And his smile...well, that smile could draw barnacles off the Coral Gardens.

So, when Aiden's name was called in the waiting room, Christel held her breath and quickly glanced over at her brother. "Do you want me to go in with you?" she asked, trying to sound nonchalant, like she didn't care one way or another.

Aiden reached for his crutches. "Yeah, sure. Whatever you want."

Christel jumped up from the uncomfortable arm chair and patiently trailed behind her brother as Aiden followed the nurse down a short hallway. She stopped and held a door open. "Right in here," she directed, motioning for them to go on in. The name plate mounted on the wall acknowledged the office belonged to *Dr. Mattisse, Orthopedic Surgeon.*

"Have a seat," she said, pointing to a set of chairs in front of a polished wood desk. "Dr. Matisse will be right in."

While they waited for the doctor, Christel couldn't help but scan the framed photos on the credenza behind his desk. One shot was of Dr. Matisse on a cruise ship standing with a group of people, laughing. In another, he was on the beach holding a surfboard. Yet another showed him leaning against a sports car with his arms folded.

No woman or children appeared in any of the photos. A good sign.

Before she had a chance to consider the matter further, the door opened again and in walked Dr. Matisse, carrying a chart. The minute he spied her sitting next to her brother, his face broke into a wide smile. "Well, hello again."

She nodded demurely, like some female fop straight out of a Regency novel. Her face grew warm as she responded. "Hello to you, too." The words came out a little high-pitched. *Seriously, what was wrong with her?*

Over the course of the next twenty minutes, Dr. Matisse went over the results of Aiden's most recent set of X-rays. "You're making great progress," he reported. "If you keep this up, you'll be able to start rehab soon."

"How long?" Aiden pressed.

Dr. Matisse told him he had to be patient. "A femur break is typically one of the nastiest fractures we encounter. There are many stages to the healing process. You are currently in what we call Bony Callus Formation, which typically occurs between days eleven and twenty-eight. After that, your bone will start to remodel until eventually, you are weight-bearing again. That is when we start rehab."

Aiden groaned out loud. "I thought you said soon. Sounds like that could take months."

Dr. Matisse nodded sympathetically. "It might, but I have every reason to believe you are on the fast track in terms of healing. You are young, fit, and you're extremely motivated. That will all serve you well."

Christel cleared her throat. "Uh, what exactly will his rehab entail?"

Dr. Matisse rubbed at the side of his chin. "Well, I'm going to be frank. Rehabilitation after a femur fracture surgery, especially one as complicated as Aiden's, will often be a slow and cautious process. Here, let me explain." He wheeled a film viewer to his desk and turned on the LED lights. He unsheathed a large film from a buff-colored envelope and fastened it in place. "See right here?"

Both Christel and Aiden nodded.

"It was extremely unfortunate that you had a break in two places. Here," he pointed. "And here." He looked back at them. "We had to surgically place a rod to properly effectuate our repair."

He flipped the light off and returned to his seat behind his desk. "As you know, your initial physical therapy treatments focused on controlling pain and swelling with the use of ice and electrical stimulation treatments before you left the hospital. When we start you on rehab, your treatments will focus on range of motion without putting excessive strain on your broken bone or the torn ligaments in your ankle. As the bone heals, muscle-strengthening exercises will be added to your regime as well as additional range of motion exercises and balance training. This will continue for up to six months."

The doctor's gaze turned to Christel. "Until then, it looks like you are in good hands. You have a very supportive family."

She felt her heart race a little as he continued to look at her. She let herself return his smile.

Dr. Matisse clasped his hands together. "Any questions?"

Aiden shook his head. "No, I think you just about spelled it out. I'm not going to say I'm happy about all this, but I'll do anything it takes to heal and get back to work as quickly as possible."

Dr. Matisse looked pleased. "I don't see any reason you can't return to work, at least part-time, once the rehab specialist tells me you're at a point where I don't think being on that leg for extended periods will put the process in danger."

"Oh, that's good to hear!" Aiden told him.

Dr. Matisse turned to Christel. "By the way, apparently I was in your neighborhood recently. I attended a dinner party a few nights back and learned the hostess was your neighbor," he told her.

"Oh?" Christel feigned surprise. "Who is that?"

"Maggie Donovan. I believe she said you live right next door to her."

"Oh, yes. I know Maggie. She's a sweet lady."

"And a great cook," he added. "Admittedly, I was a little disappointed when she told me she had invited you but you had other plans."

Christel's heart began beating so hard she was afraid everyone in the room would hear it. "Well, maybe we could ask her for a re-do."

Oh, my goodness...had she really just said that?

He smiled warmly. "I'd like that." He paused, glanced over at Aiden, then back again. "Or, perhaps you'd let me take you to dinner. I know a great restaurant. Have you ever eaten at Ko in Wailea?"

"Yes, love it," she told him. "The Pan-Asian food is incredible." *And so are the prices,* she thought.

"How about Friday night?"

"This Friday?"

Dr. Matisse nodded. "Will your schedule allow that?"

Christel tried not to answer too quickly. She didn't want to seem anxious. "Uh, yes. Friday should work."

Dr. Matisse stood. "Great, I'll pick you up at six."

Christel and Aiden stood as well. Aiden positioned the crutches under his arms. "Thanks for everything, Doc. I really appreciate it."

"My pleasure." Dr. Matisse held his office door open.

Christel started for the door, then paused. "One thing," she said, mildly breathless.

"Yes?"

"What is your name? I mean, your first name. I don't know your name."

Their eyes locked and held, chemistry surging in waves. "Evan," he said.

"Evan" she murmured. "Okay, then. I'll see you Friday."

She caught her brother out of the corner of her eye. He was grinning.

"Looking forward to it," Evan said.

Christel moved through the door, a slight smile playing on her lips. Dinner out. With a good-looking man. A smart man...a doctor, even.

There were many reasons to grow hesitant. She hadn't dated for years. She hadn't even entertained the idea of another man since Jay. If not careful, she could talk herself right out of this.

But for some wonderfully insane reason, she believed the upcoming evening with Evan Matisse might be just what the doctor ordered.

11

Aiden made his way across the stone decking surrounding his mom's pool and slipped into a wicker chair. He leaned his crutches against the edge of the table and watched Willa dive into the pool. "Nice form," he called out when her head reappeared above the water.

Katie reclined in one of the pool loungers on the other side of the pool. She lowered the book in her hand and pushed her sunglasses up on her head. "Yes, you're looking good, Willa."

"Thanks," Willa said. She swam across to the steps and climbed out, grabbed a towel and dried herself off.

In the lounger next to Katie, his mom tossed her book aside and stood. "You guys ready for some more drinks?" she asked.

Katie waved off the offer. "No, you stay put. I'll get them, Mom." She pointed to the mesh-sided play pen. "Would you watch Noelle?"

"Of course," Ava answered before turning to Aiden. "So, your sister is really going out on a date?"

"Hey, wait for me. Don't discuss until I return," Katie called out.

Ava glanced at her watch. "Okay, but don't be too long. Christel and I agreed to meet with Mig to review our fencing needs."

One of the biggest threats to a pineapple field was wild pigs. If they got into a pineapple crop, they could eat a football-field-size amount of fruit in one night. Pali Maui had to go to extraordinary effort and expense to avoid that kind of financial hit.

He shifted in his seat sending a sharp pain up this leg. He winced.

"Oh, honey," his mom said. "Are you in pain? Do you want me to get you some pain medicine?"

"No," he barked, shaking his head. "I'm not taking any more of that stuff."

His mother frowned. "Well, if you're in pain—"

"I said I'm not taking any." Aiden immediately realized his tone was a bit harsh and apologized. "It's just that I want to wean myself from all that stuff so I can go back to work."

Katie returned from the kitchen carrying a tray of tall glasses filled with a frozen concoction of bananas, coconut and mangoes. "I added little paper umbrellas." She grinned. "And a little rum in mine." She winked. "Mom?"

"Oh, no alcohol for me," Ava said. "As I mentioned, I have to go back to the office."

Willa sat on the pool steps and pulled her wet hair into a knot at the nape of her neck. "I'll drink hers," she offered.

"Nice try, but you get a virgin drink." Katie held the tray up to her mom.

Ava thanked her and took a glass. "Okay, now that you're back, let me get this clear. Christel is going on a date? With Dr. Matisse?"

Aiden nodded. "Yep. I was right there when he asked her out."

Katie moved to the table and offered him the tray. "Okay, we need details. What did he say? What did she say? And did she look excited? I mean, this is big. She's pretty much been a hermit for two years."

Willa hopped from the pool and walked over to join them, leaving a trail of water dripping from her wet suit. "Gosh, Mom. Why don't you just be nosy?"

Katie tossed her daughter a look. "Oh, stop. I am not being nosy. I'm just...interested."

"Oh, yeah?" Willa rolled her eyes and grinned. "Whatever."

"Who's nosy?"

They all turned to find Christel walking toward them. "Hey, Mom," she said. "Just wanted to make sure you didn't forget our meeting with Mig." She glanced between all of them with suspicion. "Okay, what am I missing here?"

"They're talking about your love life," Willa spilled.

Katie jabbed her elbow into her daughter's side. The sudden motion nearly caused her to drop the tray. She rallied and held out the tray to her sister. "Drink?"

Still watching them, Christel slipped one of the glasses from the table and took a sip. "Okay, clearly you were chatting about my upcoming date. For the record, and to reiterate what my savvy niece said, quit being nosy." She winked at Willa who grinned back at her.

Aiden held up open palms. "For the record, I wasn't taking part in this discussion."

Katie nearly dropped the tray. "Yeah? How did we find out in the first place if you didn't tell us?"

Ava laughed. "Busted."

Katie placed the tray on the patio table. "Is it true? You're going out on a date with Dr. Matisse?"

"We're going out to dinner," Christel clarified.

"Sounds like a date to me," Ava teased.

"It's a date," Aiden stated. "There were definitely romantic sparks in the room."

"Oh, stop," Christel told them. "My romantic life is not up for discussion." Despite the serious admonition, she was clearly pleased at the turn her romantic life had taken.

Ava placed her arm around her oldest daughter and squeezed her shoulder. "Well, you look happy. We're all very excited for you."

Katie made her way back to her lounger and picked up her book. "So, what are you going to wear?"

Before Christel could answer, a car engine pulled her attention to the circular driveway. "Hey, that looks like Ori. I haven't seen him since—" She let her voice drift off.

Aiden knew what Christel was going to say. Ori had been scarce ever since they all discovered his sister had an affair with Lincoln. Alani had told his mom he was having a really hard time with his sister's indiscretions. In that, the Briscoes understood exactly how he felt.

Aiden forced a bright look on his face. He and Ori had grown up together and had been close friends. He grabbed his crutches and stood. "Well, I'm glad he's here."

Ori cut his engine and got out of his car. He waved in their direction as he approached. Aiden could easily see the apprehension as Ori made his way to them.

Alani's son was like one family. Ava immediately went and gave him a big hug. "So glad to see you."

He looked at the ground. "Yeah, sorry it's been a while. It's just that—"

"Hey, bro. No worries." Aiden hobbled over, pulled his friend close and thumped him on the back with an open palm. "Good to see you."

Ava grabbed a drink from the tray and pushed it into Ori's hands. "Come. Sit."

Time nearly got away from them as they talked and caught

up. Ori was still busy as the director of Ka Hale a Ke Ola Resource Center. Right out of college, he helped start the outreach that served hundreds of meals to elderly and needy individuals each week.

"You been catching any waves?" Aiden asked.

Ori looked at Aiden's leg. "More than you. I mean, how are you? Sorry I didn't make it up to the hospital." A look of embarrassment crossed his face.

"Again, no worries, man." Aiden let out a small laugh. "You can make it up to me, though."

Ori's eyebrows lifted. "Yeah? I mean, anything, man."

"Let me catch a ride with you to the station. I want to check on things."

His mom immediately protested. "Oh, Aiden. Are you sure that's a good idea?"

"What? How is my going into work for a little while any different than sitting around here? It's not like I'm going to go on a rescue mission or anything," he argued.

Without waiting for any response, he looked at his buddy. "You up for it, Ori?"

Ori glanced between he and his mom. "Uh, sure. Maybe we can stop and catch a beer after?"

Aiden's face brightened. "You got it."

An hour later, they pulled into the Maui Emergency Management Administration parking lot. Ori cut the engine. He helped Aiden out of his car and together they moved for the front door.

Inside, the place buzzed with activity, even more than usual. Jeremy Hogan came out of Captain Dennis's office holding a coffee mug in his hand. Aiden's coworker immediately spotted him. "Hey, what are you doing here?"

"Just thought I'd drop by and check things out," Aiden said. "I'm not sure if you've met Ori Kane." He nodded toward his buddy.

"Oh, sure. We all met last summer when we climbed up to Na'ili'ili-haele Falls. You had that good-looking chick with you."

"My sister," Ori stated, again looking a bit uncomfortable.

"That was your sister? Whoa...well, I'd like to meet your sister again some time."

Ori shifted on his feet. "She's no longer on island."

Disappointment flashed on Jeremy's face. "Ah, too bad."

Captain Dennis popped his head out from his second-floor office door. "Hey, I thought I heard a familiar voice. Glad to see you, bud." Aiden's boss descended the metal stairs and crossed the concrete floor to join them. "Hope you're doing all those exercises they put you through in rehab. We need you back here."

"Yeah, I'm working toward that goal," Aiden told him. "I want to come back as soon as possible." That statement was far truer than he cared to admit, even to himself.

Aiden looked around the familiar space, taking in the lockers where their fire uniforms hung, the bins holding their gear and shelves lined with helmets. Hooks lined the wall filled with ropes and tethers and wenches. Near the back of the station were two parked rescue vehicles, one a firetruck, the other an emergency medical vehicle that contained a heart defibrillator, a tank of oxygen, and other emergency medical supplies.

Metal stairs led to an upper floor with a railed deck overlooking the station. That's where the offices were located—Captain Jack's, the one that housed Mike Carr, the human resources guy, and his own. He'd worked hard and was proud to have attained a management-level position. The effort had taken him nearly three long years, but was worth every class, every sleepless night, every sore muscle. No one outworked him. No one was better at this job. He saw to that.

In no time, his other coworkers learned he was there and

gathered to greet him, including Megan McCord. "Hey," she said. "You're back."

"Well, not entirely," he admitted. "I'm still finishing off some rehab. But don't worry. I'll be back and suiting up with the guys in no time." Did she notice he'd intentionally left her out of that picture?

She narrowed those pretty eyes. "Well, that's good to hear."

Aiden was in the middle of more introductions when, suddenly, the overhead alarms rang out. Beepers on the guys' belts went off. A large light mounted on the metal rafters flared and rotated, sending a beam of red light circling the interior of the station signaling an emergency situation.

Captain Dennis pulled his radio from his belt and scanned the digital display. "Looks like we have a possible drowning in Kanapali." He glanced at the assembled bunch and waved the team to the emergency vehicle. They all grabbed their rescue gear, bolted across the cement floor, and climbed into the truck. The glass-paned garage door lifted. The siren whined on as the vehicle raced out of the station and down the highway.

As soon as they'd cleared the station, the overhead alarm and lights stopped.

"Wow," Ori said, shaking his head in amazement. "That's some high-adrenaline stuff."

Aiden stood there, feeling like the kid whose mom forgot to pick him up after school.

Ori noticed. "You okay, man?"

Aiden ran a hand through the top of his hair as he balanced on his crutches. "Yeah, sure." He turned to face his friend. "Hey, can I ask another favor?"

"Sure, what is it?" Ori asked.

Aiden nodded in the direction of the upper floor. "Help me get up those stairs. I want to check on a few things in my office."

"Oh, I don't know, man. That doesn't sound like a very good idea, with your leg and all. I mean, you could fall."

"Not if you help me," Aiden assured him. He jabbed his crutches onto the concrete, took a step—then another and another—until he reached the bottom of the stairs. Ori was right behind him. "Here, hold these," Aiden instructed. He handed off the crutches, then turned and sat on the bottom step. With his arms, he lifted himself carefully to the next upper step, and the next.

Ori followed close behind. "You're crazy, you know that?"

When they reached the top, Aiden raised himself, grabbed the railing and balanced on one leg. He retrieved the crutches from Ori, secured them in place under his arms and headed for the office down at the end of the metal walkway.

About halfway, he turned around. "You coming?"

Ori nodded and followed.

As Aiden reached the open door, he looked inside. Immediately, his eyes widened. "What the hey...?"

"What is it?" Ori asked.

Aiden couldn't believe what he was seeing. The office no longer resembled the place he'd left behind. Gone were the framed commendations, including the photos of him getting the Mayor's Award last year. The walls were no longer gray, but had been painted a shade of light blue. None of his belongings were on the desk, or the credenza. Even the office chair was different.

"What the—?" he repeated, shaking his head in disbelief.

Ori looked confused. "What's up, man?"

Aiden spotted a leopard-print pencil holder filled with multi-colored pens. He quickly maneuvered himself behind the desk and yanked open the top desk drawer. "Oh, man...she even has mascara in here."

Aiden felt a surge of anger and looked up at Ori. "That little witch has moved in."

Ori raised his eyebrows. "Who? The good-looking girl? The one with the radical tats running up her arm?"

Aiden's jaw stiffened. "Yeah, that one."

He tried to think of how best to say it, but in the end, there was no blurring, no lead-in for something like this. There was only the truth.

"Megan McCord may look good on the outside, but I'm telling you right now...that woman is rotten to the core."

12

The doorbell rang and Christel immediately filled with anxiety, feeling even more nervous than when she was getting ready. She'd almost phoned Dr. Matisse and called the evening off. After pulling her phone out to do just that, a tiny voice in the back of her mind reminded her that this day was an eventuality...there would have to be a first date if she was ever going to have a relationship again. The fact was, Jay was now her past. She must look to her future.

The doorbell rang a second time, pulling Christel out of her head space. She hurried for the door and opened it. "Hello," she said, with a nervous smile.

"Hey," he said. His eyes took in her dress, a cute wrap-around with ruffles at the sleeves and along the hem—a look that was a definite departure from the casual apparel she normally wore.

The way she saw it, tonight was a night to try new things. She'd even found a cute pair of cork wedge sandals in hot pink that matched the tropical print in the dress. Katie lent her a pair of matching drop earrings that pulled the look together.

"You look really nice," he said. "I hope it's still appropriate for a guy to mention that kind of thing." He laughed nervously. "You never know these days."

"Thank you," she said, smiling. "Complimenting a woman never goes out of style. And you look…different." Seeing the look that crossed his face, she quickly clarified. "I mean, I've only seen you in a white lab coat." He wore a linen sports jacket over a white button-down and tan chinos. Something Jay would never wear. It looked good.

She invited him inside "Would you like a glass of wine?" she offered.

Christel pulled a chilled pinot blanc from the refrigerator and lifted two wineglasses from the cupboard. "So, Maggie tells me you only recently moved to the island?"

"Yes, it was a good move. I work a lot of hours and it's nice to have such a great area to enjoy on those precious time away from my practice and the hospital."

They moved out to her lanai where they continued talking, mostly about his work and the hospital. She learned he was an army doctor who served in Iraq. Prior to moving to Maui, he'd spent a year at a base in Texas.

"It was far too hot there for me," he told her. "Besides, it was time for me to try civilian life. I'd served my country and now it was time to focus on what I really wanted to do."

Christel took a sip of her wine. "And Maui was what you wanted to do?"

He nodded. "Took a vacation and loved it. The whole tropical thing was a refreshing change to the heat of Iraq and Texas, so I decided to retire my commission and stay. After a little research, I found the island lacked a good orthopedic specialist, which provided the perfect opportunity. I invested what I'd saved while in the army and opened my practice." His eyes nearly twinkled. "Haven't looked back."

"Well, our family is extremely grateful you were here to

help Aiden after his accident." She held up the bottle. "More wine, Dr. Matisse?"

"Evan," he corrected. "If we're on a date, you have to agree to call me Evan."

She nodded, slightly embarrassed. "Of course."

"About the wine...I'll pass. Our reservations are at eight." He placed his empty glass down on the side table. "And I'm driving."

Christel smiled to herself. It was nice to be with a man who knew how to place limits on his alcohol consumption. It was also nice to be with a man who was this easy to talk to.

They chatted for a while longer. A lot of small talk. The kind you exchange when you don't know the other person very well yet. He asked how she liked the neighborhood and she went into great detail about all the pluses. "Of course, there are a few minuses. The area tends to be primarily affluent older people. Not many neighbors my age. But then, I work all the time, so that's not really an issue." She wondered what Maggie might have told him about her. Her neighbor tended to overshare. "I'm a lawyer and a CPA. Like I said, I'm rarely home, except in the evenings. I guess we have that in common...the working, I mean."

Christel realized she was babbling. She was nervous still, sure. But the thing that was scrambling her brain was Evan's cologne. Scientists say that scent is one of the strongest memory triggers. She totally believed it. Every time she caught a whiff, she was immediately catapulted back in time...to mornings when she'd creep up behind Jay in the bathroom and give him a surprise hug. He had a habit of standing naked before the mirror while he brushed his teeth and put on his cologne.

She remembered feeling wholly and completely alive back then. Could she ever find that again?

Evan checked his watch. "Speaking of time, we should probably get going."

Christel stood and gathered their glasses. He followed her inside.

"I really like your place," he told her. "Sadly, I have very little furniture yet. Yours makes me want to make that a priority."

His comment pleased her. She'd known from the moment the realtor had opened the door that this house was meant to be hers. While smaller than many in the neighborhood, the living area was vaulted and an open floor plan allowed a view into the kitchen, which had a large island and upscale appliances. The real selling point was the bank of windows looking out over the lanai. Beyond that was a gorgeous view of the ocean.

"I could help you out," she offered. "I mean, I can't take full credit for how all this looks. I used the designer my mother recommended. She's very talented and seemed to hone right in on my style preferences and kept to the budget I gave her. I could give you her name."

His face broke into a smile. "That'd be great. I'm afraid I don't have much of a decorating sense."

After supplying him with the designer's name and contact information, Christel placed the glasses in the sink and together they walked to the front door. She grabbed her purse and Evan held the door open. As she passed by him, she got another glorious whiff of that cologne.

He drove a Porsche Boxster, a hot little sports car with an engine that gave Christel a rush every time Evan changed gears. She'd always dreamed of having one but had never stepped out and spent that kind of bank.

Evan seemed to note her appreciation. "Are you a car buff?"

She nodded. "I am. My dad had a vintage Jag. 1968 in frosted aqua. He found it in Bristol and had it shipped over. My mom nearly died when she learned how much he'd spent." She smiled and closed her eyes. "Ah...but I loved that car."

"Does he still have it?"

"Sadly, no. My dad tended to go through phases. He sold the car and moved on to a Midnight Express Solstice—blue—with a twin-step hull and four color-matched 450Rs on the transom. It was a very expensive purchase, and frankly, it was too much boat for him. He sold that a year later."

Evan looked across the seat at her. "Sounds like your dad enjoys the good life."

"Restless might be a better description...a person always striving for something just beyond his grasp. His best quality might've been his ability to imagine how life could be." Christel drew a ragged breath and pushed out the words she still found hard to say out loud. "He passed away six months ago."

"Oh, I'm so sorry," he said. "That's rough."

You don't know the half of it, she thought. Moments later, they turned onto the Honoapi'ilani Highway heading toward the west side of the island. About halfway to the turnoff, they drove past the large gated entrance to Pali Maui. "That's where I work." She pointed.

"Pali Maui...the pineapple place?"

She grinned. "Yes, our family owns it. We grow pineapples primarily but we grow other things too...like mangoes, papayas, and dragon fruit."

He smiled over at her—a smile as open and warm as the sun. "Tell me more. What do you do there?"

Christel explained her role. She provided all the legal and financial direction for the operation. "My mom, she's the mainstay of the operation. While I give advice, she's the ultimate decision maker. The buck stops with her." She then proceeded to fill him in on the history. "Mom inherited Pali Maui from her father. He was a huge Pearl Harbor buff and made a lot of trips to Hawaii. After my grandmother passed of cancer, he picked up his two daughters and moved them from San Diego to the island. He was a doctor as well."

"Really?" he asked with piqued interest.

"Yeah, a general practitioner. He bought Pali Mali as a tax write-off. After my mother inherited it, she invested a lot of time and money to make the operation financially solvent and what it is today." She paused, decided to step out of her comfort zone. "I'd love to show you around sometime."

He nodded enthusiastically. "I'd love that."

Evan made a turn onto Pi'ilani Highway and headed south in the direction of Wailea. Late-day sun shimmered off the surface of the ocean as they drove along the shoreline. "Sounds like to me, you have a lot of strong women in your family. I like strong women."

Christel again smiled to herself, basking in his compliment. She'd been reluctant to start dating, wondering how she could ever move forward after losing her marriage to Jay. Evan Matisse made it easier to look possibility in the eye.

They arrived at the restaurant and were seated promptly. Ko was one of her favorites and rarely disappointed. It was located at the Fairmont Kea Lani Hotel and was the Hawaiian word for sugarcane. The name was meant to reflect the many peoples who came to work Hawaii's sugarcane plantations, bringing with them their recipes and cooking techniques. The menu items still reflected that heritage.

She and Evan were seated at a table overlooking a large lanai with a view of the ocean. From here, the sunsets could be marvelous.

After an amazing dinner—Evan had the ginger Hoisin BBQ pork chop, and she ordered the seared Hokkaido scallops, followed by a delicious dessert they agreed to share called malasada, consisting of fried Portuguese sweet bread with coconut gelato topped with kula black raspberry jam—they sat for a long time lingering over coffee and talking.

Their conversation was slow and easy, punctuated by many questions.

She learned Evan grew up in Boca Raton, Florida. His folks were both still alive and had moved into the Villages, a popular retirement community located in the central part of the state.

His dad had been the high school football coach. As a result, Evan had become a star player. He was a tight-end and was offered a partial scholarship after graduating his senior year. He turned the extraordinary gift down after 9/11. "The world seemed to have turned upside down overnight," he explained. "I love this country and wanted to do anything I could to help protect our nation."

She revealed that she had wanted to go into politics, but the volatility pushed her towards law. She was still a political news buff and followed elections by flipping between channels, a habit that drove her ex-husband crazy.

"You were married before?" he asked.

Christel wasn't ready to tell him the entire story. Instead, she shared the abbreviated version. "Yes. His name was Jay Bruening." She told Evan how they had lived here in Maui while growing up and about their surprising reconnection in Chicago a few years later. "We were married soon after. Unfortunately, we…well, we grew apart and finally went our separate ways." Christel did her best to keep any sign of emotion off her face. Even now, bringing up his name was painful.

"How about you?" she asked. "Were you ever married?"

"No," he admitted. "I did have a serious relationship, while in the army. Her name was Tess."

Evan placed his elbows on the table and laced his fingers together, looking down for a moment. Then he met her eyes. "She was killed over Fallujah when the medivac helicopter she piloted was taken down by a Hellfire AGM-114, an air-to-ground missile. I was told the hit came out of nowhere. She likely never knew what hit them."

The breath left Christel's lungs. She reached for his arm. "Oh, Evan. I am so sorry."

"Bad things can happen to good people," he told her. "Tess was one of the best. Heaven was lucky to get her." He didn't tell her more, and she didn't press for additional details. It was likely there were things too painful for him to divulge as well.

After Evan paid the check, they slowly made their way out into the warm night air. To say she was stuffed when they'd finished would be an understatement. In her past dating life, she often ate very little thinking she might look fat. She felt entirely comfortable with Evan and didn't need pretend or put on airs. She could be herself. Besides, at this juncture of her life, she didn't want someone who was inauthentic or would only be impressed with her if she fit some preconceived mold. In fact, she'd proven she didn't even need a man in her life. That freed her to act accordingly.

Just outside the door, Evan turned to her. "I'm not ready to take you home," he admitted. "Do you want to go for a walk?"

She smiled. "Yes, that would be nice."

They strolled down a large concrete walkway lined with sentry and loulu palms. The air smelled of plumeria and there was a slight ocean breeze. It was the kind of island night that Hemingway wrote about, a night meant for lovers. While she and Evan were not exactly at that point in their relationship, she was enjoying the ardent attention of a male. Especially one who was so charming and good looking. The best thing? He was so easy to talk to...to be with.

He must've felt something similar because as they stepped to the edge of the bluff overlooking the waves, he held out his hand. She reached and took it, felt his strong fingers close around hers.

His touch was like a bolt of electricity. Sure, she didn't need a man, but it had been a long time since a guy had caused her heart to race. It felt good.

"I'm having a nice time," he said while looking out over the brilliant pink sunset. "I hope I get to see you again."

"I'd love that," she told him, her voice nearly a whisper. "I've had a wonderful time, too, Evan. More than I expected, really." She cleared her throat. "This was my first time out since my divorce," she admitted. "I'm glad it was with you."

If he was surprised by that disclosure, he didn't show it. He simply squeezed her hand. "Me, too."

Over the following week, they made good on the decision to spend more time together.

They went snorkeling in Parouse Bay on Tuesday morning. On Thursday afternoon, they biked the famous Haleakala downhill ride. The following day, they both arranged to be out of the office again and golfed the Dunes at Maui Lani, where she experienced her first ever hole-in-one. The amazing feat happened on the sixth hole, a little par three surrounded by water hazards.

"Oh, my goodness! Did you see that?" she nearly screamed with elation. She pumped her fist.

Sharing her enthusiasm, Evan dropped his club and picked her up at the waist and twirled her in a circle. "That was amazing," he said as he finally let her feet touch the ground.

Christel stared over at the golf green where her little white ball had disappeared into the hole. Euphoria overtook her. Was it the breathless spinning in Evan's arms, the hole-in-one? Was it Evan himself? No matter, right now she was sailing high above the world on a cloud of happy.

She glanced over her shoulder at Evan, aware he was watching her intently. He pulled on her arm and brought her closer against him. He then leaned forward until his face was mere inches from hers, his breath warm and sweet. He paused, still gazing at her face. Then he touched his lips with hers.

She closed her eyes and released herself to his kiss. Her heart pounded so hard, she was fairly certain he felt each beat against his chest.

His mouth was soft against hers. His hand cradled her

lower back. This was a man who could make her feel safe and vulnerable all at the same time. The sensation was intoxicating.

The nervous part of her relaxed. Christel kissed him back, and when she did her breathing changed pitch and so did his.

Evan cradled her head in one hand and held her firmly but gently against his mouth. She stifled a groan and swore his heartbeat was keeping up with her own.

When he pulled back slightly, Christel tried to catch her breath, to speak. "I—well, uh…"

He silenced her with his lips, his breathing heavy as his mouth slid to her neck. "Congratulations," he whispered against her ear. "That was one heck of a shot."

13

"Wait...he kissed you?" Katie's eyebrows lifted. She momentarily stopped walking, causing the treadmill to nearly throw her off the moving belt. She scrambled to regain her balance. "For real?"

Christel startled when a barbell hit the floor from across the room. Their fellow exerciser, a burly man wearing a Budweiser T-shirt with the sleeves cut off, let out an expletive.

Grinning, she glanced over at Katie with a smug look. "For real."

"Right there on the golf course where every member of the Dunes could see? I mean, so there are witnesses to this event?"

Christel rolled her eyes. "Those people are serious golfers. I doubt many were watching." She picked up her pace. "Still, it wouldn't have mattered if the whole world saw that kiss. It was a wonderful kiss. I'm not about to apologize, either, or feel guilty. I've waited a long time to feel this good again."

"No apologies necessary." Katie turned up the speed on her treadmill as well. "I do want details. What was it like?" She sighed. "I've been married so long I barely remember the first-kiss tingles."

"Long? You haven't been married that long?" Christel argued.

Katie felt her breath getting labored. "Willa is thirteen. Do the math." She wiped her brow with her forearm. "Besides, Jon is the only guy I ever dated."

Christel turned in surprise. "But you kissed others. I mean, you did kiss other guys before Jon."

Katie turned silent.

"How could you not have kissed anyone but Jon?" Christel stepped off her machine and grabbed her water bottle.

"What can I say? I knew what I wanted and was lucky enough to find the guy of my dreams without a lot of searching." Katie looked at her sister with as much confidence as she could muster. Christel had a way of looking at her...a look laden with judgment. Okay, maybe not judgment but certainly assessment. Perhaps she'd learned that in law school. It didn't matter. She didn't particularly like it. Those looks left her feeling less than her older sister.

She felt *less than* in a lot of situations. Take, for example, that time Willa came home bragging about her new teacher, the one who was only twenty-four but had multiple degrees, one from Oxford. Why a highly educated woman like that had settled for a teaching job here on the island was beyond imagination. The salary had to be inadequate for someone of her accomplishment.

And there was the rub. Almost everyone was more accomplished than her.

Katie had not finished college. She became pregnant and married Jon, vowing to not let all that intrude on her education. That was very shortsighted. She had no idea how much a new infant required. No idea how Jon's start-up restaurant would consume any ability for him to help her. No idea how sad she would feel signing the withdrawal documents.

Sure, she'd always planned to return. One year turned into

a second, then a third. Before she knew it, five years had passed. Finally, Willa was about to move into middle school and Katie toyed with the notion she might return, at least part-time. But then she became pregnant with Noelle.

Don't get her wrong. She adored her family. She would have it no other way. Still, it was a daily battle to not enter into the comparison game, especially with her accomplished older sister—the lawyer, the certified public accountant, and the all-around-know-everything-about-everything person.

A few months back, Katie had hoped to make her mark. When the opportunity presented, she stepped out and attempted a business deal on her own. Keeping the prospect to herself, she moved forward with the necessary research. She pulled together numbers and profit margins, even looked forward in time to the possibilities for expanding the deal to include international markets. While she hadn't felt entirely confident in her ability, she forced herself into a mindset that said she was capable of putting the deal together.

Securing a lucrative distribution agreement with Latham Enterprises, headquartered in Waikiki, was going to be the feather in her cap...her crowning achievement, as the old cliches went. She went to sleep at night imagining the entire scene playing out in her mind of calling her family together to announce what she had pulled off.

Sadly, the project had not gone as planned. Few things in life did. Katie had learned that a long time ago.

Katie shook off the notion and pulled herself back to the present. "So, spill," she urged her sister. "What was it like...the kiss?"

Christel beamed. She took a drink from her water bottle then screwed the lid closed. "Well, he caught me entirely off-guard. I mean, I just didn't see it coming." She closed her eyes as if recreating the scene in her mind. "But it was so good. The way his lips felt against mine. The way he smelled." She looked directly at Katie. "I'd almost forgotten how all that felt."

"Was it weird?" Katie asked. "I mean, kissing someone other than Jay?"

Christel's attention slowly drifted to the landscape outside the glass walls of the gym. "Yeah," she admitted. "Not at the time. But later."

Katie shrugged. "That's understandable. Jay was the love of your life. But it's good that you are moving on. You deserve to be happy." She meant that. Christel had never looked as delighted with life as she had this past week. Dr. Matisse had broken through that blanket of glum her sister had been under since signing her divorce decree. For that, Katie could hug his neck.

Christel tossed her towel over her shoulder and headed for the glute machine. Katie followed. She'd seen a magazine article just yesterday touting how the machine was the secret hack to help women get extra bubbly butts. It might be too late for her to get a bubbly butt, but she thought she wanted one.

"So, how's things with the unbearable neighbor?" Christel asked.

Katie adjusted the bumpers then lowered onto the padded bench seat. "Well, his grass is at least a half foot tall. I swear, the guy doesn't own a mower. I wanted to call the City of Wailuku and report him."

"Why didn't you?"

"Jon wouldn't let me. He thought the better approach would be to act neighborly and go over and mow the lawn." Katie got mad all over again just thinking about how Jon was always giving the creepy man a pass. "I said absolutely not. We kind of got in a skiff about it, actually."

Her sister grinned. "Let me guess. Jon gave in and let you have your way."

Katie lifted her chin. "No," she argued. "We simply agreed to call a truce and not do anything. At least for now."

They directed their attention and silently focused on their leg lifts. When finished, they moved on to the stationary bikes followed by the rowing machines and then they headed for the showers.

Christel opened her locker and pulled out her bag. "Great session."

"Yeah, Workout Barbie. Try asking me about it tomorrow when I can barely walk." Katie believed in regular exercise and made it a priority, but working out at the gym was not her favorite form of keeping in shape. She much preferred biking or walking or swimming. Somehow those activities didn't hurt so much. Plus, they were outdoors—not in some room with pounding music and the smell of sweaty bodies.

"By the way," Christel said as she pulled the headband off her hair. "Have you seen Shane lately? Mom says he's gone a bit AWOL."

"Well, first...this isn't the military, Sergeant Christel. Second, he often forgets to check in." A hint of a smile played at the edges of her mouth. "You know our little brother. He's always off having fun somewhere. Shane rarely stops and thinks 'Oh, I haven't called my sisters lately.'"

"Yes, I know. But Shane has been even more distant than normal. Mom and Aiden haven't heard from him lately either. In fact, I'm not sure any of us has seen him since Aiden's accident. I worry he's still struggling with losing Dad and all that came to light."

Katie ran a comb through her hair and leaned in to the bank of mirrors above the sinks to check to see if her mascara had smudged. It always seemed to migrate when she exercised. "The one you should be concerned about is Aiden. Dad was his hero and the pedestal now stands empty. Couple that with Aiden's forced hiatus from a job he loves and he's got to be feeling pretty low these days." She stopped talking, stared in the mirror. "You don't think Shane is missing that girl? What was her name?"

"Which one?" Christel barely hid the sarcasm from her voice.

"That girl who waited on us at Charley's. You know, after the ballgame?"

Her sister nodded. "Oh, the blonde."

"Yeah. Shane stayed with her longer than any other girl. That's saying something," she noted.

Christel couldn't hold back her laughter. "So, what...our brother dated her for two weeks?"

Katie waved off her comment. "Oh, stop. Mom said he liked her."

Christel pulled a bottle of shampoo from her bag. "Yeah? Then what happened?"

Katie turned on the faucet, rinsed her hands. "Shane told Mom she had aspirations of becoming a star and moved to Los Angeles."

Christel turned and gave her a pointed look. "Well, of course she did."

14

Falling in love was nothing like Shane expected. He'd watched plenty of Star Wars movies and it was apparent that Han Solo fell for Princess Leia over time. Initially, their relationship was rocky and didn't break into a full-blown boil until the big kiss scene in The Empire Strikes Back—the fifth movie in the series.

Slow was not his experience. No, he'd fallen hard...and fast.

He met Aimee Battista at Charley's while out for breakfast with his brother and sisters after a ballgame. She was hot with long blonde hair and even longer tanned legs. A short while later, he saw her again at Black Rock when he was there cliff diving with friends.

Aimee was fearless and bold. All the guys thought she was really hot. More than one were mentally lining up hoping for some Netflix 'n' Chill.

The amazing thing?

She ignored the rest of those bruhs and chose him. Admittedly, his heart was lost the minute she grinned over at him and leapt off Black Rock. He'd followed her into the water... knowing from that moment he would follow her anywhere.

He'd hooked up with Aimee for weeks. Every minute with her was truly lit. He'd never met a girl like her...someone he wanted to spend time with. He'd even imagined a future. While he didn't know what that might look like—certainly not marriage or anything—he'd hoped they would remain hooked up for a long time.

That's why the night she showed up at his door telling him she was moving to the mainland was a surprise...a bad, sick surprise.

He would never tell anyone, but he really missed her. In fact, he must have it bad because he couldn't seem to think of much else since she left.

He'd slip into bed at night and smell her on his pillow. He'd climb into the shower the next morning and picture the last time she was in there with him. He couldn't even go to Starbucks without remembering the day she showed up at his door with a double espresso with pecan whip and a bag of egg bites she'd copped off some dude she'd dated.

Shane wasn't even jealous. He loved that about Aimee...the way she wasn't trapped by all the rules. That freed him up as well. He could just be himself.

Truthfully, he loved every moment with her. Now she was gone.

Shane glanced at his watch and grabbed his T-shirt from the bed and slipped it over his head. He was late again. Uncle Jack was going to flip out. Worse, he'd cut his pay.

He was right.

"Where the dickens you been, boy?" Uncle Jack stood on the dock motioning for him to hurry up. Shane could see the raft was already loaded with tourists and he'd held them up.

"Sorry," he shouted as he climbed aboard.

His uncle gave him a brief chastising look as he positioned himself at the wheel and revved the motor. The raft slowly backed away from the dock leaving a trail of exhaust fumes.

Captain Jack, as he was known on the island, was a hulk of a man. The locals had nicknamed him Santa of the Sea, and for good reason. Not only did he sport a big belly, but he hadn't shaved in years, resulting in a long gray beard hanging well below his chin. His face was ruddy from time spent in the sun, or perhaps from drinking too much rum. He had puffy cheeks the size of small apples and a gold-capped tooth that glinted when the sun caught it just right.

While on the way out to the designated snorkeling spot, Captain Jack's voice boomed loudly and mingled with the sound of the engine. "You are riding on a hard-bottom inflatable vessel known as Canefire. This raft is one of the safest vessels on the water. She's even rescued Coast Guard boats in trouble," he claimed in his gravelly voice. He patted the dash. "Yup, Old Grandma has to save the grandchildren once in a while."

Shane moved to the port side of the raft and opened the lid on the wooden equipment box. He pulled out multiple sets of fins and handed them out to the passengers.

"Today, we're heading to the backside of Lana'i to what's known as Shark Fin Rock. I've seen almost everything there while in the water...whales, dolphins, turtles, whale sharks, manta rays, a blue marlin, and lots of octopus." He popped an unlit cigar into his mouth and grinned. "Should be a great day!"

That's when Shane saw her—standing there at the front of the boat with the wind in her short-cropped hair and a body that filled out her bikini in all the right places. She smiled at him, an invitation of sorts.

He smiled back and headed over to help her with her fins. He leaned down and helped her foot into the opening, taking his time to appreciate her long and very tanned legs. When finished, he straightened. "Here, let me," he said as he checked the strap on her face mask. She lifted her hand and brushed her fingers against his bare legs...a clear message.

A quick image of Aimee formed in his mind. Just as quickly, it vanished. She was gone...it was time to move on.

15

Evan Matisse enjoyed the pace of his practice in Maui. While he had no lack of patients needing orthopedic care, his schedule here on the island allowed for pau hana—a more relaxed approach to practicing medicine. Here, he was his own boss. Sure, patient needs would always dictate his work schedule, but he no longer answered to military command.

Contrasted with the army, life here on the island was a cake walk. Not only was the environment incredibly lush and beautiful, the people were olu'olu'. He'd never encountered folks who were so friendly.

Evan cracked three eggs into a bowl and whisked them. He pulled his favorite pan out and melted some butter, then poured the eggs inside the pan and adjusted the heat.

Except for emergency situations, he did surgeries on Tuesdays and Thursdays. Patient appointments were on Monday, Wednesday, and a half-day on Friday. He was on call at the hospital every other weekend. This left time for an occasional afternoon at the beach or on the golf course.

Life here was a one-hundred-eighty-degree turn from

serving in the military, especially when he was deployed to Iraq. Doctors working in an environment of armed conflict faced situations where patients had overwhelming injuries with limited access to medical resources to provide appropriate treatment, especially in orthopedics. Often service men and women had to be transported to Germany by medivac...at least those fortunate enough to survive their injuries long enough for that option. And the doctors themselves could be in danger. He, of anyone, knew how the stress of all that could suck a person dry.

His time in the Middle East, and all that happened there, had left him empty. Depleted. Sort of used up. That was ridiculous for a guy in his mid-thirties. He should be planning his future, not feeling drained.

Even when he'd had enough of overseas and returned to serve Stateside, he couldn't seem to fill that deep hole in his spirit—the chasm that formed from all the times he'd had to declare a situation futile, knowing that a mother, a father, perhaps a wife, were going to be forced to feel what he had in losing Tess...the deep pain and loss of knowing the end had come. There would never be another *see you later*. No more phone calls. No more shared meals. For those who were married, no more shared beds...or quick morning showers with the one you cherished.

Evan opened a bag of shredded cheese and pulled a pack of sliced mushrooms and some bacon bits from the refrigerator and laid them on the counter before checking the pan of eggs.

One thing no one could dispute—his deployment had made him very good at two things—the practice of medicine and hiding his inner pain. No one knew the toll those months had taken. Or the guilt he still struggled with.

Evan ran the spatula around the omelet pan. When the egg mixture was sufficiently loosened, he lifted the pan from the burner and gave his wrist a quick flick. The omelet flipped to the uncooked side. A perfect maneuver.

Perfection was paramount. Any miscalculation could be costly. Losing Tess had taught him that.

He placed some cheese in the center of the eggs along with the bacon bits and mushrooms. Seconds later, he folded the omelet in two and grabbed a plate from the cupboard and slid the hot omelet from the pan onto the surface.

After pouring himself a glass of grapefruit juice, he wandered out to the lanai with his iPad tucked under one arm so he could catch up on the news while he ate. He sat and placed his napkin on his lap, said a quick blessing, and dug in.

He had a busy day ahead after taking a few days off.

Spending time with Christel Briscoe had been worth the backlog. He'd dated some in the past two years, but no woman had captured his attention like this one. He couldn't entirely put his finger on why, only that there was something. Like a magnet, the pull was strong. While he'd tried to argue himself out of it, he'd felt an instant attraction that day in the hospital when she flung her arms around him. It was the most personal touch he'd shared with a woman in a long time, and he wasn't going to deny how much he enjoyed it. He'd nearly had a visceral reaction to a woman's arms around his neck again. And not just any woman...*her*.

The time they'd spent together was surreal. He hadn't felt that carefree since before his deployment to Iraq. She was attentive without being clingy. She was smart and witty, could carry on detailed conversations about business, about politics, and about life. He admired that, while she'd encountered loss, she hadn't allowed the experience to diminish her positive outlook.

Evan felt a stirring within as her image formed in his mind.

She was gorgeous. Not in a flashy sort of way but attractive without trying too hard. Hazel-green eyes. Skin tanned and flawlessly smooth. He couldn't help noticing how her blonde hair was cut in a fashionable style with short wisps that playfully brushed her jawline. Each time her eyes twinkled and she grinned, her smile illumined the room.

And that kiss! The moment his lips touched hers something electric rippled through every cell of his body. Another thing he'd not felt since Tess.

Evan downed his juice then scraped the last of the omelet from the plate and shoved it in his mouth, unable to quit thinking about her.

Christel loved football. And her family. And cars.

She had a knock-out body, tall and curved in all the right places. She was athletic, had definitely out-surfed him. Her golf swing was enviable. She was surprisingly ardent about her political positions, yet more than willing to carefully consider other points of view. He could spend hours talking with her. From the first night at dinner, he knew he'd found someone special.

Christel Briscoe was the first woman since Tess to make him want to open up and reveal more...to have more than simply cooking and eating an omelet alone.

So, that begged the question...why hadn't he told her?

16

Ava secured her Bible on her lap and settled in to listen to Elta's sermon, wishing her children would attend with her. Like Lincoln, they often elected to take a pass on regular church attendance, a decision that didn't sit well with her. She let out a heavy sigh. Look what skipping church had done for Lincoln's moral character.

Next to her, Alani smiled in adoration at her husband. Their steadfast commitment to one another was heartwarming. While she could no longer claim that for herself, she wanted her daughters blessed with men who were totally abandoned to them.

Katie and Jon had a steady relationship, though they both worked far too much. If she could point to anything she may have contributed to Lincoln's wandering, that had been her downfall. She too often placed work above time with him.

Through no fault of her own, Christel had experienced the heartbreak of a crumbled marriage. Some relationships were not salvageable—especially when your spouse was hell-bent on self-destruction.

Her budding relationship with Dr. Matisse was a nice turn

of events. Never had she seen her daughter's face so bright. Clearly, her daughter thought a lot of him and was enjoying time with him.

She wanted good marriages for her boys as well. Aiden and Shane had a lot of life to experience before settling down, especially Shane. Someday, they would make some lucky girls very happy.

Ava gazed at the soaring ceilings and magnificent stained-glass windows in the church, at the beautifully carved wooden pews. She felt at peace here.

Alani leaned over and whispered, "What you thinking about?"

Ava couldn't help but smile. As hard as her best friend argued to the contrary, she often slipped and phrased her sentences in a manner that revealed her native heritage.

She lowered her voice and answered. "That life is good."

Alani reached for her hand and gave it a squeeze.

After the church service was over and the congregants had disbursed, Alani motioned to Elta. "Hey, honey. Ava and I are going to slip out and do some shopping this afternoon. I left Polynesian meatballs in the refrigerator. You only have to pop them in the oven for twenty minutes. Use a covered dish," she reminded.

He leaned and kissed her plump cheek. "Thank you, sweetheart. You go and have a good time."

On the way to the car, Ava remarked about how thoughtful Elta was, how he rarely put up a fuss whenever his wife had anything planned. Alani waved her off. "Yes, but even more... my man loves to have the house to himself so he can take a Sunday afternoon nap."

The drive to the Shops at Wailea took less than twenty minutes. Ava parked, and she and Alani made their way through a courtyard filled with palms and outdoor tables. The area was known for being one of Maui's premier shopping and dining destinations, home to more than seventy boutiques, shops, restaurants ,and galleries.

First stop was the Louis Vuitton store. She selected wallets for Christel and Katie, a wildly extravagant purchase she planned to give them for no reason at all. Alani raised her eyebrows as she stood beside her at the purchase counter.

"Lincoln's life insurance policy," she noted. "The way I figure, I deserve to be a little outlandish with those funds."

Alani didn't argue that. "Well, if that's the tactic here, we should also hit Prada."

Ava grinned. "Nah, I got it out of my system already."

Next, they wandered into Cariloha, where she bought a cute beach towel for Willa, a round one lined with hot pink fringe. She found a little sundress for Noelle in Mahina, where Alani found the perfect sun hat. "The sun is a killer when it comes to my complexion," she claimed.

She chose board shorts for the boys at Ripcurl then wandered into Quiksilver and couldn't resist purchasing them a second pair along with Monkey Wrench sandals. She loved spoiling her kids, especially Shane, who never seemed to have excess funds.

She followed Alani out of the store. "Where next?"

"How about we go somewhere and you buy something for yourself?" Alani suggested. "Kahuna Nui Hale Kealohalani Makua."

"Help me out on the translation?" Ava had lived on the island many years but still couldn't translate all of Alani's sayings.

"It means *Love all you see, including yourself.*" Alani gave her a pointed look. "You always forget to love yourself." She grabbed Ava's hand and pulled her along. "Let's go to a jewelry store and you find something for you. Something pretty."

"Oh, I don't need—"

"Nonsense," Alani argued. "Use those insurance funds for something dazzling."

They made their way to Greenleaf Diamonds, a popular jewelry store. Ava went reluctantly, Alani with much enthusiasm.

The glass cases were filled with beautiful bracelets, pendants, watches and rings. They browsed for several minutes before Alani let out a screech. "Here...this!"

Ava sighed and wandered over. Her best friend pointed to a large emerald-cut yellow diamond surrounded by small white diamonds with a price tag that nearly made her eyes pop. She immediately shook her head. "Oh, no. I don't think so."

Alani stomped her foot. "It is perfect." Without waiting for Ava's consent, she motioned the sales clerk over. "She'd like to try this, please."

The suited gentleman nodded. "Ah, yes. One of our best pieces." He pulled the ring from the display case and held it up to the light so the stone flashed its brilliance. "Yellow diamonds are very sought after," he told them. "Yellow is a color that represents knowledge, intellect, and wisdom. A yellow diamond ring symbolizes the beginning of a life living happy and in love."

This only caused Ava to become more reticent. "Thank you, but no."

Alani bumped her shoulder with her own. "Try it on," she urged. "You are living happy, despite everything that has happened. And you will find love again, hoaloa."

It was true, through determination and effort, she was finding happiness. She doubted she'd ever find love again...and she didn't want to.

Alani leaned close. "Ooh, it's gorgeous! And just your size." She parked her hands on her ample hips. "Ava Briscoe...if you don't buy this ring for yourself, I'm never going to make you haupia again."

Ava groaned. Haupia was a coconut custard dessert made with corn starch and cut into little squares. Alani knew it was her favorite and the one thing she requested for her birthday each year.

She groaned. "Ah, friend...you should go into politics. You are very good at spending other people's money on frivolous items that have no merit when it comes to sensibility."

Alani laughed at that. "Sensibility is highly overrated."

Minutes later, they exited the store arm-in-arm with the new ring on her finger. They made the twelve-minute drive to Monkey Pod, a trendy restaurant they both adored. They shared a hamakua wild mushroom and truffle oil pizza and an order of lobster deviled eggs. They topped it off with homemade root beer that was to die for.

Alani wiped her mouth with the corner of her linen napkin. "So, how's the thing going with Katie and her neighbor?"

Ava rolled her eyes. "Well...from what Jon tells me, he has to hold my daughter back nearly every day. Otherwise, she'd pop his head off."

"Goodness, I thought leaving his furniture in their driveway on moving day was fairly bold. What else?"

Ava told her about him filling up their trash receptacle and how he neglected his yard. "It's quite the eyesore," Ava reported. "Or, so Katie says. The latest is that he ran his hose across her grass and hooked up to their water spigot."

"Wow. That is crossing some boundaries. Sounds like he has a lot of nerve," Alani noted.

Ava couldn't agree more. "Well, you can only imagine how Katie is dealing with it. She wants to egg his house, except she's an adult and an action like that would set a poor example for her children." She laughed. "She did march over and bang on her neighbor's door a few times. Gave him a tongue-lashing of the sort only Katie can deliver." They both laughed at that.

"And Jon?"

Ava reached for a second slice of pizza. "Well, Jon is far more accepting of his bad behavior. He thinks the guy's actions aren't worth getting in a rift over."

"What if the situation escalates?" Alani asked, concerned. "Jon might want to rethink things and make a firm point now, before that happens."

Ava couldn't agree with her more. "As you know, my son-in-law is known for avoiding conflict at all costs...a trait that has served him well being married to my high-strung daughter."

Alani reached for her glass of root beer. "Ori dated a girl like that once. She was much worse than Katie. They'd only dated a few months and she broke things off with him." She leaned over the table a little. "Frankly, I think she couldn't see herself in a long-term relationship with a guy who ran a non-profit. She had higher aspirations and a longing for a larger bank account."

Ava nodded, thinking about how only months ago, the next topic of conversation would move to Alani's daughter, Mia. Now, they both knew better than to bring her up. The hurt was too fresh.

Instead, Ava waved the waiter over. "Could you bring us a slice of that fresh strawberry pie? And two forks?"

Alani held up an open palm. "You are not helping out my diet."

Ava's phone buzzed and she pulled it out of her purse. She raised her eyebrows. "Hmm...it's Jon. He rarely calls." She swiped her finger over the answer button and drew the phone to her ear. "Hello?"

"Mom?" The trembling voice coming through the phone was her daughter's. "I just got a call. Our house is on fire!"

17

Jon and Katie raced to his SUV and tore out of Pali Maui, leaving skid marks on the pavement. Jon muttered a curse under his breath and reached for Katie's hand. Her eyes filled and her heart pounded. "Can you drive faster?"

When they were a few miles from their house, Katie suddenly remembered Noelle was at daycare. Would she be able to pick her up on time? "I'd better text Willa and have her pick up Noelle."

Jon agreed that was a good idea. "Yeah, don't tell her anything else. Not yet."

Minutes later, they were forced to pull to the side of the road as sirens behind their vehicle blared. Two large firetrucks raced by. Immediately after, Jon pulled back out onto the road and gunned the engine.

"Jon, hurry!" Katie urged.

Her husband drilled her with a look, angry that she had the nerve to push him to go faster when, clearly, he was already speeding.

As they passed the supermarket where she typically purchased her groceries, memories formed.

The down payment for their house in Wailuku was a gift from her parents. On closing day, her mom had surprised them with a yard filled with garish plastic flamingoes and a sign that said *Welcome Home.*

She could recall walking up the sidewalk with a tiny bundle in her arms, fresh from the hospital, twice. And the bedroom upstairs where they'd made those babies. The living room flashed in her mind where Jon spent long nights assembling Barbie houses for under the tree on Christmas morning. She could see herself in the kitchen baking brownies for Girl Scouts and saw the shower where she and Jon spent time in order to get some privacy. He'd tease her that too much noise might wake their girls.

Tears welled in her eyes. Their family photos. Jon's prized cookbooks. Their entire life was in that house.

Jon turned onto their street. From there, they could see flames. Katie's hand flew to her chest. "Oh, Jon."

As they neared, Katie spotted some of Aiden's team from Maui Emergency Management Administration. On the island, each township had its own fire department. MEMA members still showed up and offered assistance.

Jon barely parked before Katie flung her door open and scrambled from the car. She raced toward their yard and was immediately stopped by a girl with a tiger tattoo on her arm. "I'm sorry. You can't go any closer. It's too dangerous."

Katie wanted desperately to wiggle free of the girl's hold on her arm. It was *her* house and it was on fire. Jon stood behind her and placed his hands on her shoulders. "It's on fire," he muttered, not believing what he was seeing.

Of course, it was on fire. The flames and the acrid smell of smoke testified to that. She reached for one of his hands and squeezed, feeling her throat swell with emotion. She could barely breathe.

A car rushed up and screeched to a halt. Out climbed her mother. She circled the front of her car and helped Aiden from the passenger side and together, they rushed over. "How did it start?" her mom asked, her voice loud enough to be heard over the shouts of the firefighters and the whining sound of another hose being unreeled from a firetruck.

Jon shook his head. "We don't know yet," he yelled back.

Aiden hobbled closer using his crutches. He was stopped as well by the woman with the tattoo.

"Move," he shouted.

She held up her open palm. "Afraid you're off duty." She pointed to his leg. "And injured. It's not safe."

Despite being on crutches, he pushed her away. "I said move," he repeated.

Suddenly, an explosion from inside an upstairs window sent small pieces of debris raining down in the air. "Back," one of the firefighters shouted. "Everyone back."

A dog barked from behind a fence several doors down. "Oh my, God," Katie yelled. Her gut pulled in on itself. "Givey is inside!"

She yanked away from Jon and raced past her mom. The girls would never recover if their beloved pet came to any harm. Neither would she. She had to get Givey.

Determined, she slipped past a line of firefighters who were concentrating on the flames, including the woman who had asked her to stay back earlier, and barreled toward the front door.

Aiden followed, though slower. "Katie, stop. It's dangerous!" he yelled.

She had nearly reached the front step. Smoke billowed through the doorway where the front door had been broken down by the firefighters. Each smoldering breath seared her lungs. She placed her forearm over her nose and mouth to keep from choking and blinked several times in order to peer inside.

The flames had made their way from upstairs to the banister of the staircase. Through the open doorway, she could barely make out the furniture inside.

The fire was terrifying. Her eyes burned from the smoke, sending tears streaming down her cheeks. Even from here, she worried her hair might go up in flames. "Givey!" she called out.

Someone grabbed her, pulled her back. "No! You can't go in." She turned and it was Captain Dennis, Aiden's boss at the station. With his gloved hand, he patted a spark that landed in her hair from the second story.

Katie sobbed. "Please, I beg you. I've got to get our dog!"

"Katie, no. You can't go in," Jon told her, grabbing and pulling her tightly against his chest. He too was in tears.

Before she could move to free herself, a figure appeared inside the house coming from the direction of the kitchen... their nasty neighbor, Spud Weaver. He stepped from out of the smoke, his T-shirt blackened. His face was red and swollen and smeared with soot. Sweat poured from his forehead.

In his arms, was Givey.

18

Shane tugged on the thick mooring rope and tied it off on the dock. Despite battling a colossal hangover, he'd done his duty and pulled himself from bed at the crack of dawn so he could join his uncle for a sunrise excursion on the Canefire.

It always astounded him that people were willing to get up that early on vacation, especially with the time lag many of them wrestled. As the day progressed, they'd taken out four more tourist groups—two snorkeling trips to Lana'i, a run to Molokini where tourists got a kick out of swimming in a sunken volcano crater teeming with fish, and two trips to secret spots his uncle knew of where the shoreline was lined with hono turtles. Little kids, in particular, loved this tour.

Shane hated the work but loved the money he was making. Partying could be an expensive proposition when women were involved. Some of the girls he'd hung with lately liked dinner and drinks in hotel restaurants. That's what he'd really liked about Aimee. She was satisfied with spending time on the beach with friends.

When Shane finished securing the vessel, he walked to the

other side of the raft where his uncle, known as Captain Jack, held out his bear paw of a hand to help an older woman step off the boat and onto the deck. She gave him a grateful smile. "Thank you. We had so much fun." She slipped a wad of bills into his hand, then turned to Shane and did the same. He grinned with gratitude.

A preschool-aged kid hung back and started screaming, "No, I want to stay on the boat."

His mother took hold of him firmly and told him if he quieted down, they'd go for some Dole Whip. "No," the kid protested. "I want shave ice."

Shane rolled his eyes, not sure he'd ever want to be a parent.

His phone buzzed and he pulled it from the waterproof bag clipped to a loop on his board shorts and lifted it to his ear. "Hey, Mom," he said. "What's up?"

"Honey, I thought I'd best call you before you saw it on the news. Jon and Katie had a house fire this morning. I'm afraid there's a lot of damage. The upstairs is gone and the downstairs suffered severely from the smoke."

"Wait. What?" Shane scowled in disbelief. "Mom, is everyone okay?"

"Yes," she rushed to assure him. "Willa was shopping with a friend and Noelle was at daycare. Both Jon and Katie were at Pali Maui when they got the call."

"Man, Mom. That's awful about their house. Do they know how the fire started?"

"No, not yet," his mother reported. "The crazy thing is that her neighbor—the one she detested—well, he went inside and saved Givey from the fire. Risked his own life."

"Wow. That was major decent. Guess the old guy wasn't as bad as Katie thought after all. So, what will Jon and Katie do now? Do they need anything? 'Cause I can help."

"I'm sure they're going to need all of our help eventually.

For now, they'll move in at Pali Maui and use the vacant worker's cabin. We'll have to clean it up and stock it with linens and supplies, but it'll do temporarily. An added plus is that Jon and Katie will be right here and close to the restaurant and the gift shop."

"You mean the shanty?" Shane had called the worker's cabin the *shanty* from the time he was little. "Yeah, I'm sure my sister will love that. It's pretty cramped for all four of them plus a dog." Shane glanced at the ticket counter where another line was forming. With one hand on the phone, he jumped back in the raft and started organizing the snorkel gear.

"Well," his mother said. "I urged them to join us in the big house but Katie declined. Aiden offered up his house as well. She thought Lahaina was too far from Willa's school. I'm sure it'll work out. Besides, they'll rebuild fairly quickly, providing their insurance company cooperates."

Despite his sister's tragedy, Shane couldn't help but laugh. "Let's recap. I live in the loft above the packing sheds. Aiden is staying with you. Katie's moving into the shanty. Maybe Christel will move home and then we can call it a full house."

KATIE CLIMBED from Jon's car, exhausted. "C'mon, everyone. Mom has dinner waiting, and we all need some sleep."

"Dad, what about clothes?" Willa asked. "I don't have anything to wear for tomorrow." Her voice sounded weepy.

Jon drew his daughter into a shoulder hug. "We'll go first thing and buy you and Noelle all new things. It'll be fun. You like to shop."

Katie understood how her daughter felt. She was weepy as well. It had been a long day. Their home had suffered a lot of damage. The entire upstairs was gone except for a corner of Noelle's nursery. The downstairs was scattered with blackened debris, was water-soaked, and had significant smoke damage. Jon thought it might be a total loss.

The idea that their home was gone made her shoulders ache. On top of her already busy life, she now had to find a new place for her family to live? While the worker's cabin, or the shanty as Shane called it, would work temporarily, she'd have to search for a rental. Then they'd have to rebuild. A project of that magnitude would consume her. How would she possibly juggle it all?

"I'm starving," Willa said as she headed inside. "I hope Grammy Ava has something good to eat."

Katie's mom greeted them with hugs. "You must all be so tired. I have grilled cheese sandwiches and tomato soup waiting." She cupped Willa's chin with her fingers. "Your favorite."

After dinner, they all dropped into bed. Katie was surprised that sleep did not come quickly. With her head nestled against the pillow, she stared at the ceiling in the dark. "Jon?" she whispered. "Are you awake?"

"Yeah," he muttered back.

"Hold me?"

He reached and drew her against him. Katie folded her arms around his shoulders and nestled her head against his chest.

"I was wrong about Spud," she admitted. "I mean, he was a pill for sure, but when it came right down to it, well..." Her voice drifted off as she considered what could have happened had their neighbor not played the hero.

"Yup, people can be surprising sometimes."

Katie nuzzled even closer, feeling shaky and overwhelmed with all that had transpired. An unwelcome thought tiptoed through her mind. "Jon, what if the fire had broken out earlier, when we were all in our beds asleep?" An involuntarily shudder ran the length of her back. She squeezed her eyes shut and concentrated on her breathing, ignoring the misbeats of her ragged heart at the thought her family might have perished.

Jon pulled her tighter. He stroked her hair. "We weren't there, babe. We were looked after."

Katie wasn't a particularly religious person. She attended church occasionally, especially when her mom put on the pressure. Embracing the notion someone else was in control of her life—someone she couldn't even see—well, believing didn't come easy.

Maybe Jon was right. Maybe God had looked out after them. They'd lost material things but they were all safe. Thanks to Spud Weaver, that included Givey.

She pressed her face against Jon's chest and took a shaky breath, struggling to let go of the emotion she'd carried all day. In that moment, she remembered the why and how of her love for him. Jon was her rock. Her steady place when her bruised vulnerability got the best of her.

There, in the arms of her husband, she finally cried.

19

Shane eased his Jeep up to the curb and shifted into park. The rhythmic rattle of the engine filled the air as Aiden climbed out. Rain drummed against Aiden's back as he turned and leaned down. "Thanks, bro."

His younger brother strained his neck and looked at him through the open passenger side door. "You sure you don't want me to help you inside? You might slip on the wet pavement."

Aiden shook his head. "Nah, I got it. I won't be long. Pick me up in about thirty minutes." He positioned the crutches and made brisk, swinging steps across the parking lot to the entrance of the station.

He wished everyone would stop treating him like an invalid. He was sick to death of being laid up. Sick to death of putting his life on hold and more than tired of being dismissed and shoved to the back of things because of his injured leg.

Yesterday, at Katie's house and the fire, he'd felt useless. His sister's house was burning and all he could do was stand on the sidelines and watch while the firefighters and his team took action. He might be mild-mannered, but he'd had enough.

He had a reputation for being a Jake, someone who was

cool under pressure. Even in the most severe situations. How many times had Captain Dennis expressed he was the epitome of what he looked for in an emergency worker?

He wasn't doing anyone any good sitting on the sofa all day. He'd made great strides and could now walk short distances without his crutches. It was time to get back into action.

Shoving his angst deep inside, he paused at the entrance and leaned his crutches against the doorjamb. Taking a deep breath, his hand opened the entryway glass panel and he moved with cautious slow steps and went inside.

He'd been fervently working the routines in rehab, had followed all the orders. He'd returned to the hospital for a multitude of follow-up tests and X-rays and met with Dr. Matisse for consultations regarding his progress. While cautiously optimistic, his surgeon was pleased and advised walking full-time without crutches was only a few weeks ahead.

He wasn't waiting.

Grant Costa looked up from where he stood painting an equipment box. "Hey, bro. What are you doing here?" He wedged his thumb and finger in his mouth and let out a high-pitched whistle. "Hey, guys. Look what the cat drug in." He took a look at Aiden's hair, wet from the rain. "Dude, you look like you've been out in the surf."

Slowly, his team members filtered from where they were working, some from the kitchen and others from under the open hood of an emergency vehicle. Jeremy Hogan wiped his hands on a blue rag and stuffed the corner in his back pocket. "Hey, glad to see you, man. Sorry things turned out the way they did at your sister's house yesterday. Bad break."

Aiden concentrated against wincing with pain as he stood with a hand outstretched. He greeted his team members then glanced in the direction of the upstairs offices, including his office, which had been invaded by Megan McCord.

She appeared in the doorway, waved, and scrambled down

the metal steps to join them. "Aiden, I'm surprised to see you. I thought your mom said the doctors had ordered you off your feet for a few more weeks."

That girl had a lot of nerve acting so matter-of-fact. She thought she knew everything about everything. A classic narcissist. Very early, he had his suspicions about her...none of them good.

The guys seemed to shift on their feet and look away. While they'd never discussed the matter, the guys likely completely agreed with his assessment.

"Sorry," he told her. "You must've gotten it wrong. I'm coming back tomorrow. I'm just here to let Captain know."

And to give you time to vacate my office, he thought.

Trust between the team members here at Maui Emergency Services was a part of their culture—the department's DNA. Trust was key to safety and performance. It was imperative to successful execution of their IAP—incident action plan.

Of course, this had not been an overnight process. Aiden had played a big role in helping to foster that trust and had learned that trust involves risk. You have to let go before you are 100 percent certain of the outcome. Every new team member has to be allowed to step up and do the job, supported with the belief in their abilities rather than cripple them with doubt or micromanagement.

He might be young, but he had a good head on his shoulders and had earned the respect of his team members and management alike.

Megan McCord would never earn his trust.

"So, I need to alert Captain that I'm returning," Aiden said as he walked toward the stairs.

Megan followed close behind him. "Captain is out. He should be back shortly," she said, her voice a bit cryptic. Just what was she hiding?

At the end of the open balustrade, outside his office door,

stood a stack of cardboard boxes. They were taped and written in large letters on the side in black marker it read: *Aiden's office*.

He felt a rush of pure, blinding anger. Why, that sneaky, conniving...

She quickly moved in front of him as if to block his view.

"What's going on?" he demanded. Without waiting for a response, he maneuvered around her and pointed. "You boxed my things?"

She rubbed at the back of her neck. "It's not what it looks like..." She let her words trail off.

That's when he saw the new name tag on her uniform top. 'MEMA Team Liaison.'

His job!

He crossed his arms against his chest. "Yeah? Well, I'll tell you what it looks like. It looks like you're a lousy opportunist who jumped at the chance to weasel herself into my job while I was out recuperating. Did you think I wasn't coming back?" He felt a stab of anger, so swift and sudden, it shook him. "Did you think I wouldn't fight back?"

He wasn't some pushover and Megan McCord was going to learn that very soon.

"Aiden." A familiar voice caught his attention and he turned toward the stairs to find Captain Dennis approaching. His boss swiftly closed the gap and placed his hand on his shoulder and grabbed his other hand for a vigorous shake. "This is a surprise."

Aiden's eyes narrowed. "Yeah, I've heard that a lot today," he muttered.

Captain Dennis grinned. "Well, we weren't expecting you today, but I'm glad you're here. I have an announcement."

Here it comes, Aiden thought. The big *I'm handing your job over to a woman who is not as qualified and hasn't even been here two minutes.*

A thought occurred. She likely filed with the human

resources department at the City of Maui complaining of gender inequity or some such ludicrous notion. Forced the captain's hand into making a move he didn't want to make.

Aiden was supportive of women. For the most part, he felt there was no difference in judgement or abilities between males and females. He was a fan of making sure all employees had equal opportunity. But, given the circumstances here, Megan's promotion smelled foul.

He sincerely wanted to rattle her cage and shake her up. Send the message that he had her number and her actions weren't adding up.

Captain Dennis got on the loudspeaker. "Attention everyone. I have an announcement to make. Five minutes...conference room."

Aiden's heart grew heavy as he stuffed his true feelings and told the captain how happy he was to be coming back. Not only that, his leg hurt like the dickens. It hadn't been the brightest idea coming here today. In fact, nothing had gone as expected.

While Aiden was on his extended medical leave, Captain Dennis had obviously been forced to replace him.

Aiden began rehearsing his options. He hated to leave MEMA but what choice did he have? He wasn't about to work under that woman.

The options here on the island were slim, but surely, he could find some way to put his skills to best use. He wanted a career that mattered. He'd fully expected to spend years here at MEMA. In what seemed like a moment, everything had changed.

When they'd all assembled in the conference room, Captain Dennis moved to the head of the long rectangular table. "Well, I'd planned to do this a little later. Given Aiden is ready to come back sooner than later, I guess there's no time like the present." He cleared his throat. "As you know, Maui Emergency Management has grown in size over the past five years. Our incident count is up, surpassing all projections. We've had to work harder, and smarter."

Captain Dennis's face grew somber. "That is why my decision came only after serious and anguished deliberation." He looked across the room at them all. "I'm resigning my position as your captain, effective as of the first of next month."

A collective sense of shock crossed the room.

"What do you mean?" Grant asked. "You can't leave."

Captain Dennis chuckled. "Oh, I'm afraid we're all expendable. In my case, I've been here for nearly thirty years. My wife is telling me I need to retire so we can spend time with our grandchildren. My kids and their families all live on the mainland—Montana and Ohio. At first, I was reluctant to give in. After some thought, and careful consideration, I knew Edie was right. No one knows more than the people in this room that the unexpected can occur at any time. None of us is promised tomorrow."

Aiden frowned. "I—I don't understand," he muttered. "What about the team?"

Captain Dennis smiled at him from where he stood. "Well, son. That's where you come in." He looked around the table, delight spread across his face. "I'm incredibly pleased to announce that the position of captain is being awarded to Aiden Briscoe." He winked at Aiden. "If he accepts it, that is."

The guys all scrambled over to him. They patted his back and shook his hand. "Congratulations," Grant said, grinning.

Jeremy echoed the same. "Couldn't have picked a better man." He gave Aiden a hearty wallop on the back. "Captain Aiden. That has a nice ring to it."

Aiden stood there, stunned. He was going to be made captain?

That's what this was all about? Why his office was packed up and Megan had moved in and now had his former job?

He swallowed and dared to look across the table at her.

Megan stood with her hands on her hips and a wide smile plastered on her face. "Welcome aboard, boss."

There were few times in his life where he felt like nothing but a heel. Right about now, the shoe fit and he had no choice. He was going to have to wear it.

20

Christel grabbed her cup of coffee and headed out to the lanai. Was it just her imagination, or was the sky a more vibrant shade of blue this morning? The sun a little brighter? The air in her backyard a little more laden with the scent of mango and coconut?

Everything seemed sharper and more ebullient these days.

She slipped into the cushion of the wicker chair and took in the view of the turquoise ocean in the distance knowing there could only be one reason...Evan Matisse.

Christel felt like a schoolgirl again. Her stomach filled with that buzzy sensation when she thought of him—which was far more than she would admit to anyone. She went to bed thinking about those light green eyes and the way his neatly trimmed beard was peppered with gray. Her dreams were filled with that surprising moment on the golf course when his lips had moved onto hers...the way he felt against her, the taste of him, the smell of him.

Sometimes, late at night, she lay in bed unable to sleep and would imagine Evan in the empty space beside her, flashing that brilliant smile and whispering in her ear.

Like a schoolgirl, she carried her phone with her at all times…in case he called. When he did and she saw his name appear on the screen of her iPhone, her stomach did flip-flops.

She even went shopping for the first time in a long while. Katie was more than willing to help her pick out some new tops and jeans, and a couple of new swimsuits and coverups. She did her makeup and spritzed on her favorite cologne every day, even on weekends…just in case he texted and wanted to come over.

The entire experience was heady and unnerving all at the same time.

While she couldn't bring herself to entirely pull Jay's image from the sturdy mental frame she'd carried with her since the divorce…now, finally, she'd found herself able to slip another man's picture in front of his.

She couldn't help but grin.

This just might be the first sign that a newly improved Christel Briscoe was beginning to rise from the ashes.

EVAN WALKED into his office bright and early on Monday morning, still basking in the weekend spent with Christel Briscoe.

Evelyn looked up from her computer at the front desk. "Good morning, Dr. Matisse. How was your weekend?" She leaned forward slightly and grinned. "You look very relaxed. I hope you got to spend time with that nice Ms. Briscoe."

"Yes, a nice weekend," he answered, avoiding commenting on his social life. "A weekend without emergencies is rare. Guaranteed, I took full advantage."

"I hope you got rested because it's going to be a busy Monday. We have a woman on her way who fell off a kitchen stool. Sounds like she may have broken her hip. I sent her directly over to the hospital and alerted X-Ray."

"Thanks, Evelyn." He turned for the hall leading to his office. "I'll check on a few things and then head right over. Hopefully, nothing is torn and the poor woman can get away with anti-inflammatories and icing. Maybe a shot of cortisone." While Evan was a surgeon, he tried to avoid surgical inventions whenever possible.

"That's not all," his receptionist said. "The nurse in emergency called and gave a heads-up. There was a diving accident at the Westin in Ka'anapali. Some teens goofing off and one slipped and hit the diving board with his shoulder. The EMTs called it in and said looks like a bad break."

He nodded. "Hello, Monday morning. I guess all good things must come to an end."

Evan headed for his office with the time he'd spent with Christel over the weekend still on his mind.

On Friday night, they'd gone to dinner at Fleetwood's on Front Street in Lahaina. The eatery was owned by the legendary rock-n-roll legend, Mick Fleetwood of Fleetwood Mac fame, and featured rooftop dining that offered fabulous oceanside views and the best seafood chowder around.

Saturday had them both up and out of bed hours before dawn. He picked her up and they made the drive up the Haleakala Highway to Leleiwi Overlook where they joined dozens of tourists watching the sunrise. The experience, especially shared with Christel, was nearly spiritual. As they stood at the summit, he wove his fingers with hers as the distant horizon slowly broke into shades of apricot, yellow, and pink, then burst into mango orange before splashing the sky with bright sunlight.

On the drive back down the mountain, they stopped at the Ali'I Kula Lavender farm. He never knew so much could be done with the fragrant flowering herb...lavender chocolates, brownies, scones, coffee, lotions, lemonade, candles, pillows, and more. They feasted on a treat of Earl Grey Lavender Crème brulee for breakfast...not exactly a healthy meal, but a sweet delicacy they both enjoyed with a dark, rich cup of coffee.

On Sunday, they attended church with her family. The pastor at Wailea Chapel was a close family friend of the Briscoes. Evan enjoyed meeting Elta and his wife, Alani, and their son, Ori and was surprised to learn Alani ran Te Au Kane luau.

He also discovered that Aiden had not exactly followed the doctor's orders when it came to remaining off his leg. Evan had a lot of patients like that...ones who jumped the gun and wouldn't stay down as recommended. In Aiden's case, he felt the bones were sufficiently healed to withstand his patient's impatience. So long as he didn't overdo it, he assured Christel when she expressed her concern.

On the drive home after church, he left the top down on his Porsche and gunned the engine, sending the wind through Christel's blonde hair. He loved the way the light caught in the strands.

She noticed him staring and smiled. "I've never felt like I've known a man so well in such a short amount of time, and yet not at all," she admitted. "It's like I've known you for years, not weeks. Yet, I find myself wondering about so much."

"Like what," he asked.

Christel shrugged. "Nothing...and everything." She paused.

He grinned. "If you want to know something, all you have to do is ask."

Christel thought a moment. "Okay, what about this. What are three things you want to do before you die?"

"What do you mean...like a bucket list?"

She nodded. "Yes. What are the things you long to do or see? I'll go first." Christel quickly ticked off her items. Her dreams included a trip to Washington, D.C. "I've been several times," she told him. "But someday I hope to observe a session of oral arguments before the U.S. Supreme Court. An issue of national significance with brilliant constitutional attorneys making their cases. Second, I'd like to eat my way across southern Italy and bottle my own wine, a vintage classified *Denominazione di Origine Controllata e Garantita*, the highest designation for an Italian wine."

"Wow, you dream big," he commented, chuckling.

"Like my dad used to say, go big or go home." Christel gave him a sideways look, and Evan couldn't help but admire the intensity in her eyes, the way every emotion was displayed in the deep pools of green.

"And, what is your third?" he asked.

"Oh, that's easy. I want to fall in love again." The admission seemed to startle her. She immediately looked away.

Evan reached and took her hand in his own. "I want that, too," he admitted.

"Your turn," she urged. "Name your bucket list items."

He thought a long moment. "When I was in Iraq, I saw a lot of limbs lost to explosions. And sadly, other more severe and life-altering injuries. I was flipping television channels a couple of nights ago and came across a documentary featuring a doctor here in the U.S. who recently made ground-breaking medical history by performing the first successful face transplant. My specialty is orthopedics, but I'm fascinated with the idea of a procedure that is so transformative...a medical miracle, of sorts. I'd love to meet the surgeon and assist. It's a far stretch, but since we're dreaming big, why not?"

"I love that!"

"Second, I'd like to...okay, promise not to laugh?"

"Of course, I won't laugh," she quickly assured him.

"Someday, I want to ride a bull in a rodeo. Preferably in the Calgary Stampede."

Christel's eyebrows raised in surprise. "What? Now, that is

entirely out of character. I can't even imagine you in cowboy boots and a hat. What prompted that dream?"

He laughed. "Probably stems from all the John Wayne movies I watched with my dad while growing up."

"Sounds like you were close."

He thought a moment. "Yes, we were. I miss him very much. He had the rare ability to push a person to do their very best, yet gave room for falling short. No judgment ever."

Christel reached and squeezed his hand. "And, what's your third?" she asked.

Evan hesitated, worried his admission might scare her off. "I'd really like to be a dad, too, someday."

What he didn't tell her was that he'd had a son...a son who was never born. A son who went down with Tess in the helicopter. Or, that his death, and that of his mother's, was his fault.

21

Katie tied the balloon and reached for another. "What do you mean, Evan got a strange look on his face?"

Christel tore open a package containing a congratulations banner. "I mean, we were sharing our bucket list items and he said he wanted to be a dad someday."

Katie pulled the balloon to her face. "That's a good thing, right?" She puffed her cheeks and blew into the balloon.

"Yeah, sure. It's hard to explain, but he got this really distant look and...I don't know, kind of clammed up for a while."

Katie shook her head and looked heavenward. "You over analyze everything, Christel. I'm sure it was nothing."

Christel shook her head. "I'm not so sure. I—well, I think he was hiding something."

Katie lifted her eyebrows. "See? There you go again. Classic Christel."

"What?"

"You haven't dated since Jay. Now it sounds like you're sabotaging." She tied off a filled balloon, then grabbed another and pulled it to her lips and blew.

Christel huffed. "I am not. Besides, a lot of guys out there have issues."

Katie dropped the balloon to her chest, fingers squeezing the end tightly to hold in the air. "Their issue was that you hid out at work. Like I said, you need an Overthinkers Anonymous meeting."

"And I think you need a life."

Katie looked at her with patience. "Look, sis. You're never going to find anyone who doesn't have baggage."

"Yeah, but hiding it isn't cool." Christel took the balloon and tied it for Katie.

"Well, you're one to talk. You haven't been exactly forthcoming with the reason for your divorce. Or, how losing Jay broke your heart."

"That's different," Christel argued.

"Really? How?"

"Because..." She paused. "The reasons for my divorce are not relevant to this new relationship. What happened back then is between me and Jay."

"So, you'll never tell Evan the details?"

Christel carefully folded the banner. "Perhaps someday, if the relationship gets serious and I don't *sabotage* it."

Katie slowly nodded. "Isn't it heading in that direction now?"

Christel waved off her comment. "Oh, you know what I mean."

"Mommy...I got *poop tastes*." Noelle toddled into the kitchen clutching a tube of toothpaste in her chubby little hand.

Katie jumped up and retrieved the tube from her daughter's fingers, unwinding the tiny but powerful digits. "Willa!" she hollered. "You have to quit leaving things down for Noelle to get into. And you're supposed to be watching your little sister."

Willa's voice came from one of the open doors down the

hall. "You don't have to yell, Mom. This house is small enough I can hear you. And I didn't leave the toothpaste out. Dad did."

Katie rolled her eyes and turned to her sister. "Of course, he did." She sighed. "I'm not sure how much longer we can live all crammed into this tiny space."

"How's the house hunt coming along?"

"It's not," Katie admitted. "We'd move to a bigger place, a rental, but everything here on the island is outrageously expensive. Any place that would work for our family also requires a long-term rental agreement. The other problem is furnishings. I don't really want to buy all new things until we're back in the house. This rebuild seems to be a perfect time to go ahead and remodel and do some updating."

Christel closed the plastic bag holding the banner and placed it in a box with other decorations. "Ugh, what are your options?"

Noelle raised her dimpled arms toward the pile of balloons. "Badoon. Badoon." Katie reached and lifted her daughter up on her lap. The tiny girl arched her back in protest. "Badoon!"

Katie kissed the top of the toddler's downy head and tried to distract her. "Are you going to wish Uncle Aiden congratulations?" Katie cooed, holding Noelle eye-to-eye and jostling her back and forth in a pathetic attempt at redirection. "He has a brand-new job. Yes, he does," she said, voice lilting. She looked over at Christel. "A little help here?"

Christel laughed and folded her arms. "You're on your own. I'd only sabotage it."

Katie sighed. "There's no way I'm going to keep this one out of the *badoons*. I'm also not sure we're going to be able to pull off this surprise party. He already suspects something is up."

"Nah, Aiden has been preoccupied with this promotion. I'm sure he doesn't expect a thing," Christel argued. "Especially since he's not actually returning to the station until next week. I told him we all wanted to go to dinner in recognition of him being the top dog. He won't expect us to be throwing a party."

Katie wasn't so sure. "I think you underestimate our brother. And I'm not talking about Aiden. Shane has been known to spill the beans, even when he's been warned to keep things quiet. Do I need to remind you about last year's surprise birthday party for Mom?"

Christel groaned. "Ugh, that's right. Well, I'll personally knock him into tomorrow if he tells Aiden what we're doing." She stood and put her hands on her hips and surveyed their progress on the preparations. "It's all looking good. What else do we have to do?"

Katie pulled her clipboard from the table which held her long list. Several items were checked off. "Invitations were mailed. Check. Groceries bought. Check. Cake ordered. Check. Decorations." She extended her hand and waved it across the room. "Check."

"What about wine? Beer?"

"Jon's taking care of that. He's also preparing the food, of course."

"Is Evan coming?" she asked.

"I invited him. Unfortunately, he has a surgery scheduled and that might make him a bit late to the party. I told him that was fine." She wandered to the refrigerator, pulled the door open. "Do you have some soda?"

Katie shook her head. "Yes. But soda isn't good for you. Cucumber water is much better for your endocrine system. I have some made in the pitcher at the back. First shelf."

"So, now you're Dr. Oz? Doling out health advice?" Christel bent and retrieved the water.

"I'll have you know I admire Dr. Oz. He's very knowledgeable."

Christel didn't take the bait, not wanting to argue the merit of television medicine. Instead, she moved to the cupboard for a glass. "Want some?"

Katie shook her head and held up her half-full glass.

"Wait, is that—? That's Coca-Cola!"

"It is," her sister confirmed.

Christel scowled. "I thought you said soda wasn't good for you."

Katie's face broke into a wide grin. "I said soda wasn't good for *you*. I'm fine with it."

"Surprise!"

Aiden's hands flew to the top of his head. His birthday wasn't until next month.

"Ta-prize," little Noelle shouted. She flung her hands up above her head. They all laughed.

"We got you," Katie exclaimed, more than pleased.

Christel stepped to him and wrapped him in a hug. "Katie didn't think we could pull it off. But that look on your face—well, looks like we succeeded."

Ava moved closer and took her son's face in her hands. "Congratulations, honey. We are all so proud of you."

"Thanks, Mom. And uh—yeah, you certainly did surprise me," Aiden told them before moving deeper into the room. "I can't believe it."

Ava's living room was decorated for the big event. Brightly colored balloons dangled from the wooden beams above the palatial living room. A banner that spelled out *CONGRATULATIONS!* hung above the open patio door slider leading out to the pool. On the kitchen island was a large sheet cake decorated with little plastic firetrucks and helmets similar to the toys he'd played with as a child. Aiden had always had a bent for being a rescue worker. Despite his recent accident, his dreams had paid off. The Briscoes had pulled out all the stops in helping him celebrate his success.

Alani and Elta drew near. Ava's best friend pulled Aiden against her ample body for a hug. "We were so pleased to hear the news, Aiden." Elta said likewise. "We couldn't be more proud and happy for you, Aiden."

Ori stood by the side of the room with Shane. He lifted his beer can. "Captain Briscoe has a nice ring to it."

Ava wholeheartedly agreed. She made the rounds, hugging necks and repeating over and over how she couldn't believe they'd pulled off the surprise. This party had caught her son completely off guard.

The room was packed with guests. Miguel was there, of course, along with many of their workers. Her brother, Jack, was out on the lanai smoking a cigar. He waved. "Can you believe our boy made captain, sis?"

There were long-time work associates and all the guys from the station, including Captain Dennis and his wife. A few of Aiden's school friends were there. Church members mingled with old friends. The room was packed. It seemed like yesterday they all feared the worst after Aiden's accident. Everyone seemed as relieved as she was to see how quickly he had healed and were delighted to hear of his promotion. They wanted to wish him congratulations.

Noticeably absent was her deceased husband, Lincoln. And Mia, of course.

Ava quickly pushed the hurt of Lincoln and his affair from her mind. This was a happy day. She intended to make sure it stayed that way.

The party didn't wrap up until well after midnight.

When the celebration was over, Jon carried a sleeping Noelle as he took his daughters back to the shanty. Katie and Christel stayed to clean up.

Aiden tried to join them in the effort but his sisters shooed him away. "The guest of honor doesn't tidy up after his own party."

"Thank you, all," he told them as he made the rounds, hugging each of their necks. The party was so very thoughtful," he told them. "You know how to make a guy feel special."

"Our pleasure, honey," Ava told him. "We love you." She gave him a final hug, happy to see how his face still glowed from all the attention. He'd been severely glum ever since Lincoln had passed, and especially after the boat accident. She was so happy to see him get the break he deserved.

Christel moved to the kitchen island. She licked the frosting from the cake knife before placing it in the dishwasher. "It was a great party, wasn't it? Nearly everyone we invited showed up."

Shane appeared in the doorway carrying a folding kitchen stool. "Hey, a little birdy told me you needed help taking the balloons down."

"That little birdy was me texting you and telling you to get your butt over here so you could help." Katie informed him.

"Me? What about him?" Shane pointed to his brother who was entering the room from the lanai.

"What about me?" Aiden asked moving with caution. He pointed to his newly healed leg. "Uh, even if I wasn't the guest of honor at this shindig, I think this gives me license to sit this one out."

"Oh, there it is. The broken leg excuse. If you're good enough to return to work full-time, you're good enough to throw away a few used paper plates and cups." Shane grinned. "I mean, if you think you're up to it. Don't do it if you think it'll tax your strength." He laughed as he opened the kitchen stool and positioned it under a group of balloons then climbed the steps to the top. "Dude, seriously. You're the expert. Rescuing all those cats from trees. I don't see how you get a pass on this one."

Aiden brushed off his brother's comment. "Oh, I think I do," he teased. "Besides, what are you? Twelve?"

"Boys!" Ava said, her eyes filled with laughter. "Do I need to break the two of you up and send you to your rooms?"

They all laughed.

Shane shook his head and reached for a group of balloons. "Wouldn't be that hard to do, Mom. Especially since nearly all of us have moved back home."

"Temporarily," Katie reminded.

"About that," Ava turned to face her daughter. "I talked it over with Christel earlier today. She said you're having trouble finding a suitable rental." She paused, looked at her daughter straight on. "We think you should build."

Katie's face blanketed with feigned patience, as if she had the beginning signs of dementia. "We are rebuilding, Mom."

Christel washed her hands at the sink. "Hear her out, Katie."

Ava slid onto one of the barstools. "I think you should build here at Pali Maui." Katie started to protest but Ava held up her hands. "Think about the added space. And the commute time both you and Jon would shave from your daily schedules. Pali Maui is still close enough to Willa's school. Best of all? The land is free."

Katie frowned. "Okay, now you're really making me nervous, Mom. You sound like a hen gathering her chicks."

Ava fingered the back of her hair. "Forgive your mother for wanting to have you all back on Pali Maui. You all loved living here. Given the fire and all, it makes perfect sense for Jon and Katie to return and build here, right, *chicks*?" She motioned to her other children to acquiesce.

Collectively, they nodded and mumbled agreement.

Ava turned her victorious gaze to Katie. "What's wrong with my plan?"

Katie looked to her sister. "Christel, tell her what's wrong with that plan. I mean, I don't see you packing up to move back home."

Christel immediately sided with her mother. "It's not a bad notion—all of us living here...you know, someday. I mean, you're right. I have my house in Pa'ia and have absolutely no plans to relocate. But the idea of you and Jon making your home back here at Pali Maui makes great sense." Christel shrugged. "Maybe one day, I'll do the same."

Aiden joined them. "Uh, this might not be a good time to break the news." He placed his arm casually around his mother's shoulder. "But I'm moving back home this weekend. I'm good...walking and taking showers, etc. It's time to return fully to my life. My house in Lahaina isn't going to remodel itself."

Ava sighed. She expected that was coming. "I suppose it is time. There's still a plot of land for both you and Shane when you boys have families and are ready to settle down."

Shane held up two open palms. "A family? Geez, Mom. You're getting a little ahead of yourself. I don't know about Aiden, but it'll be at least a decade before I'm ready to have a family." He looked over at Katie. "Not that I don't enjoy my nieces, and all. But...me? A dad?" He laughed. "I don't think so."

Headlights flashed through the windows. Ava craned her neck for a better look. "Who can that be at this time of night?"

Katie peeked out the window. "I don't recognize the car, Mom." She backed away and wiped her hands on a kitchen towel. Finished, she grabbed both ends and flipped the fabric against Christel's backside.

"Hey," her sister scolded. "Careful. You know what they say about paybacks."

The doorbell rang sending melodious chimes through the air. Ava rose from the barstool and made her way to the entrance and slowly opened the front door.

Her heart leapt into her throat.

"Vanessa?" Her face went dark. She scowled. "What on earth are you doing showing up here?"

22

"Well, hello to you too, sis." Vanessa teased as she drew Ava into a hug, one Ava didn't care to return.

"Aunt Vanessa!" Shane said as he made his way to her. "It's been a long time. Good to see you."

She grabbed his shoulders and held him out for inspection. "Oh, my goodness. Don't tell me this is that little boy I used to bring—"

"Bags of salt water taffy," he finished for her.

"You were what—thirteen when I last saw you?" Vanessa turned to the others and held her arms open. "Come here, guys. Auntie needs a hug."

Christel was the first to make her way to their surprise visitor. Katie followed and then Shane. Each let their aunt draw them into an embrace while Ava looked on with ill-disguised contempt.

"So, what's it been since we last saw you? Ten years?" Ava folded her arms at her chest. "Maybe more?"

Vanessa waved her off. "Oh, not that long surely. I'm sorry I wasn't able to make it back for Lincoln's memorial. Work, you know. I was covering the confrontation between police and protestors when they took over a six-block area northeast of downtown." She directed her gaze back to her nieces and nephews. "Regardless, we can all agree it's been too long."

"So, why now?" Ava asked.

Vanessa dug in her bag and retrieved a small envelope and held it in the air. "Aiden's party."

Ava shot a look at the girls. Christel shrugged and mouthed, "We didn't think she'd come."

It was no secret in the Briscoe household that Ava was at odds with her sister. Growing up, Vanessa Hart was the self-appointed star in the family. A stunningly beautiful dreamer adored by all who met her. Of course, they didn't really know her like she did.

If there was a club for globeheads, Vanessa could easily be president. Everything revolved around her—what she wore, where she went, what she thought—to the exclusion of all else. She started hundreds of projects, never finished a one.

Although she was wildly successful, she burned through money like a pyromaniac through paper. It was nothing for Vanessa to drop five grand on a purse just because it matched an outfit. Her shoes were from top designers—Jimmy Choo and Manolo Blahnik. Her clothes were the latest fashions straight off the runway at Fashion Week. Exorbitant vacations to Greece and Bali. All of that flash drew a lot of favors, especially from the opposite sex.

There were two kinds of people in Vanessa's world...those who likewise pasted on pretense and went to church on Sunday and those who partied with her on Saturday night.

Her sister's sexy, easy, come-hither smile guaranteed she never went without a boyfriend, sometimes more than one at a time which didn't seem to pose any long-term problem. She was known to switch men like wristwatches.

Ava could forgive all that. What she could not let pass was how she'd bailed on their father when he needed her most. It was also no surprise Vanessa hadn't made contact when Lincoln died. Weeks later, Ava received her sister's email apologizing for missing his funeral. "Zoom...I thought it would be on Zoom."

Family was disposable in her sister's book. Her own daughter, Isabelle, chose to live with her father because her mother had made her career a priority and was never there.

Her sister motioned for them all to follow her into the open living area. "Sit. Catch me up," she said. She spent the next half hour telling them all about her life in Seattle...how much she adored living in the Pacific Northwest. "People claim it rains too much. I find the weather charming. It's like being in a magical rain forest." She grinned. "Besides that, there's a Starbucks on every corner."

While Vanessa chatted with her children like the long-lost favorite aunt, Ava eyed her for a long moment. Even at fifty-two, she remained stunning. Movie star beautiful—and Ava had to wonder how much Botox was holding her together. Her deep auburn hair was pulled back in a casual manner yet had the look sported by women much younger. Nothing sagged under her brown eyes. Her lips were a pretty coral color and plump. More cosmetic injections, no doubt.

Steeling herself, Ava moved to the island in the kitchen. "Do you want something to drink?" she asked, politely and motioned for Vanessa to come with her.

Katie followed them. "Maybe you're hungry, Aunt Vanessa. We can cook you up a bite," she offered.

"No, I'm good. I had dinner with a new friend I met in the airport."

Ava bit back a mean retort. *Of course, you did.*

"Where are you staying?" Katie slid into a barstool. "And how long will you be here?"

Vanessa glanced at Ava sideways. "Well, I hoped I might stay here."

Ava quit breathing. *Here? No way!* Everything inside her rebelled at the notion.

She scanned her mind for a graceful way to decline the situation when she glimpsed a fragility that was new to her sister, a fault line running beneath the surface of the bright smile on Vanessa's face.

Still, while she certainly had plenty of room in this massive house, Ava couldn't bring herself to open her home to an unwelcome guest, even if it was her sister. Perhaps, *especially* since it was her sister.

Finding her footing after having her world pulled out from under her feet had been arduous. It had taken months to learn to live with what Lincoln had done. Until today, she'd thought it couldn't get worse. The new tension might take her under.

Shane placed his hand on his aunt's shoulder. "That's great, Aunt Vanessa." He looked at his mother. "Isn't it, Mom? We'll get to spend some time getting reacquainted." His face was beaming.

Ava nodded feebly. There was no easy way out of this one.

She drilled a look at her sister who blinked with doe-like innocence. "So, can I stay?" There was a desperation in her voice.

Ava took a deep breath, released it. "Yeah, sure. It'll be just great."

23

Ava tossed the remainder of her coffee into the sink and dropped her mug into the dishwasher while avoiding thinking about the elephant sleeping in her guest bedroom. Instead, she focused on all she had to do today.

She definitely had a full plate ahead of her. In addition to her normal activities, a media company was coming to Pali Maui to film a segment for a travel documentary they intended to release on Netflix. While she felt honored to have Pali Maui included, the interruption would pull her away from working with Christel to finalize documents the bank needed to renew their operating line for next year. It seemed no matter how fast Ava went, how hard she worked, she was always running behind these days.

She looked down and noticed a fragment of a deflated balloon near her feet. She bent to pick it up while thinking about all the fun they'd had last night. The party had been a huge success. Aiden had been promoted and they had celebrated his new position in style.

After retrieving the balloon fragment from the floor, she noticed a sticky spot on the kitchen tile. She grabbed a wet paper towel and worked to wipe it up knowing things could have turned out so differently after her son's boating accident. Despite a long and arduous recovery, Ava would always be thankful for Dr. Matisse and the surgeries that had put Aiden back together.

She smiled to herself, smugly.

Evan Matisse was her hero on many fronts. All her questions about his relationship with her daughter had been put to rest when she'd noticed the look on Christel's face as Evan reached for her hand. It was unmistakable, Christel had finally moved on from her failed marriage...a real feat since her daughter's attempts to emotionally escape had been thwarted. It was as if Jay kept holding onto her ankle.

For the first time since the divorce, Christel seemed free and ready for a fresh start...a notion that made Ava incredibly happy.

Ava tucked her smile and made one final swipe at the floor, then lifted. She glanced up and saw her sister standing there wearing a silk robe. "Oh!" she said in surprise. "I didn't realize you were up."

"Morning, Cinderella," Vanessa said. She crossed the kitchen and went about helping herself to a cup of coffee.

Ava swallowed the insult and tried to figure out what to say to a sister she hadn't seen in years. "I hope you slept well," she finally offered.

"Oh, yes. Thanks. Those open doors leading to the lanai are a nice touch. You and Lincoln have done well for yourselves." Then, as if remembering to be thoughtful, her sister added, "I'm really sorry about Lincoln." Her condolence sounded hollow and unconvincing.

"Thank you." Ava had no intention of going further with the conversation. Losing Lincoln, and all that followed, was entirely too personal to share with a stranger. True, a stranger she had grown up with, but nevertheless a woman who had morphed into barely an acquaintance.

There was a time she could never have imagined this estrangement. Yet, the split in their relationship was well-deserved, especially given Vanessa's past choices.

Ava wiped her hands on a kitchen towel and carefully folded it then placed the fabric on the counter next to the sink. "Well, I hate to do this, but I have to run. There's a lot going on today." As if to punctuate her excuse, she quickly added, "And I didn't know you were coming."

Vanessa smiled and waved her off in that dismissive manner she had. "Go. You don't have to babysit me. I'll be fine." She stirred some sweetener into her coffee. "We can go to dinner tonight. My treat."

Ava gave her a noncommittal nod. "Okay, well...I'll see you later."

In an awkward silence the two sisters stood in the kitchen, bound by the invisible threads of their history.

Ava turned to go, replaying a memory of Vanessa standing in a kitchen long ago wearing pajamas and pigtails. Funny how a single mental image could remind her of years together—slumber parties and makeovers and breakfasts spent watching Saturday morning cartoons.

Mostly, Ava remembered her sister pulling the heads off Ava's Barbies and flushing them in the toilet.

Ava pulled the door closed and crossed the portico walking in the direction of her office and trying not to feel guilty. Leaving her sister to fend for herself was definitely rude. She should feel ashamed. Yet any notion of doing otherwise made her feel even worse.

After their mother died and the family relocated from San Diego to Maui, Ava moved like a lesser planet in Vanessa's orbit. There was no doubting her younger sister had been her mother's favorite while Ava had been her father's buddy, the son he never had. After cancer won over their mother's battle, everything changed.

Without her, life lost its shape. Especially for their father, who now favored her little sister—mainly because Vanessa was the spitting image of their mom. Sure, it may have been Vanessa's younger age and the way she wailed every night that she wanted her mommy that had pulled at his heart. The end result remained...Ava felt pushed aside.

Deep down, in a dark place she rarely acknowledged, Ava hurt, too. She simply wasn't as vocal about it.

By middle school, Vanessa had come into her own. She was a cheerleader, class president, and had her pick of boyfriends. Her popularity only grew in high school. Despite a mediocre grade point average, teachers flocked to offer recommendation letters for college applications.

Her sister met a guy in her freshman year at the University of Washington, a marketing director at a Seattle television station. She lobbied for a job and he seemed to like her assets, in more ways than one. They married, and Vanessa dropped out of school, became a mother and started climbing the ladder, making her way from marketing assistant to weather girl to news anchor in a coveted time slot.

Vanessa became a media sensation. Ratings soared. The whole world loved Vanessa. Sadly, it still wasn't enough. She wanted more and made sacrifices to get it. Her family, and often her integrity, was placed on the altar of her career.

It was Ava who cared for their father, Ava who made all the decisions and took over Pali Maui and kept the operation afloat, Ava who spent sleepless nights by his bedside during those final weeks. Vanessa was nowhere to be found, claiming her life could not be put on hold without dire consequence to her career.

After their father died, and the tension that followed, years passed with little to no contact. Now, Vanessa was here. She'd simply showed up expecting to slip into the role of devoted sister and aunt, like nothing had ever happened.

One thing Ava knew about her sister was that she had a calculated purpose for everything she did.

Which brought up a very important question...why was she here?

And why now?

24

Christel looked up when her mom stepped into her office. "Morning, Mom. What are you doing here? I thought you'd be spending some time with Aunt Vanessa."

Ava moved to the coffee bar her daughter had in her office and plugged a pod into the Keurig. "Did you forget the film company will be here today?"

Christel closed out the P&L file on her computer and reached for her coffee mug. "I'm sure Katie and I could handle things."

Ava watched the dark liquid drip into her mug. "Well, maybe so. But when the producer reached out, he specifically indicated he wanted me to go on camera and explain the history of Pali Maui and what this operation means to the island of Maui and its tourism."

Christel grinned. "Oh, so that explains the cute haircut." She waved her hand in her mother's direction. "And the makeup."

"I wear makeup every day," her mom said, defending herself.

Christel raised her eyebrows. "Every day?"

Her mother's chin raised slightly. "Well, almost every day."

That made Christel laugh. Her mother was stunning even without makeup, the kind of woman who was as beautiful in a pair of jeans as she was in a gown. She was tall and fit, wore her dark hair in soft curls that barely brushed her shoulders. She embraced a simple, classic style—nothing flashy, and her pale green eyes and bright smile made her seem perpetually young.

Even more, her mom was admired for her sharp business acumen and intelligence...qualities Christel sought to emulate. Ava Briscoe was both soft and sharp, a perfect blend of Audrey Hepburn and Margaret Thatcher.

"What are you staring at?" her mother asked while stirring some sweetener into her coffee.

Christel smiled back at her. "Nothing. I just...well, I love you."

"I love you, too, sweetheart." She folded into the chair in front of Christel's desk. "Now, let's take a look at those financials and see what the bank needs."

THE FILM COMPANY showed up right on time. Ava was astounded at the number of people involved. There was a director, a nice fellow named Curtis Jackson, who wore chinos and sandals. He quickly made introductions of the crew members, which included several camera men and a number of people with clipboards described as marketing and artistic assistants. She was told a few were day players hired exclusively for this project.

Curtis pushed his glasses up into his hair. "I can't express how much we appreciate you opening up Pali Maui to us and letting us tell your story."

"The pleasure is all mine," Ava replied. "When the Tourism

Authority reached out to me, I expressed then that the exposure would be great for us. Now, what can I show you?"

"Why don't we start off with a tour?" he suggested. "That'll give the grips time to set up. We'll likely get some great shots along the way."

Ava took them to the packing sheds first. With a camera following, she described how the fruit was brought here fresh out of the fields. "This conveyor carries the pineapples through these troughs and submerges the fruit in an ozone liquid that kills any bacteria. All the good pineapple float to the top. The bad ones sink and are later composted and sold to local orchid farms for fertilizer."

Ava led them inside the shed and pointed to an area where workers in hair nets shepherded pineapples through another process. "This is where the pineapples are dipped and sealed with lime sulfur, then wax. The sulfur prolongs the fruit's life and the waxing gives a glossy shine that appeals to buyers."

Curtis lifted a megaphone to his mouth. "Cut!" He turned to Ava. "That's great. We laid down some great film, very informative."

Next, she loaded the crew members into one of the tour buses and they drove out to the fields where she pointed out various stages of planting and growth. "Nothing goes to waste. Pali Maui is extremely eco-conscious. We even grow sunflowers along the edge of the fields and use the oil to make biodiesel for our equipment."

When they got to the part of the tour where the tasting was done, she motioned for all of them to exit the bus. The cameras were set up and she pulled out a large machete-shaped knife.

Curtis pointed. "Let's get a three-shot of this."

With precision slices, Ava removed the crown and outer skin. She then carved the pineapple flesh into chunks and offered them up to the production crew. "Guaranteed, you won't find a sweeter pineapple than the ones grown here at Pali Maui."

"This is all so fascinating," an assistant commented. "I can't believe I've been to Maui on several occasions and never visited. The grounds are beautiful."

An hour later, they were back at the main offices. Ava pointed out the Market at Pali Maui. "My youngest daughter runs our retail shop and the tours. Her husband is our chef at Na Ka 'Oi." She turned to Curtis. "When we wrap up, I'd love to host your crew for a complimentary lunch. We serve—" She suddenly stopped in the middle of her sentence.

Out of the corner of her eye, she spotted her sister walking in their direction. She wore white crop pants and a hot pink top made of chiffon that seemed to flow over her shoulders. Matching earrings dangled from her ears.

As Vanessa drew near, Ava gave her The Look—the eye-to-eye signal that this was not a good time to be bothered.

Of course, Vanessa ignored her and waltzed right up and extended her hand to Curtis Jackson. "Well, hello. Welcome to Pali Maui," she said with a brilliant smile.

Ava felt something twist deep inside her.

Curtis's face dawned with recognition. "Hey, aren't you Vanessa Hart?"

Her sister placed her hand against her chest. "Why yes, I am."

He introduced himself. "I used to live in Seattle, watched you on the news every evening. I'm a huge fan."

Vanessa batted her eyes, taking in his flattery as if she wasn't used to being fawned over. "Really? Why that's so nice to hear."

"Oh, yes. In fact, my favorite was the night you reported on the South Lake Union crane collapse."

Vanessa shook her head, sadly. "Killed two ironworkers and two passersby on the street. Such a tragedy."

Curtis nodded. "But you brought the human side to the story." He looked at her with admiration. "You are very talented."

Ava fought to keep from rolling her eyes at Vanessa's feigned blushing.

The director nearly stumbled over the adoration piling up at his feet. "So, you're here at Pali Maui because—"

Before Curtis could complete his question, Vanessa jumped in with a response. "This is our family operation."

Ava fisted her hands by her sides. "I think what she's trying to say—"

Now it was her turn to be interrupted. Ignoring her, the director waved over his camera man. "Do you mind?" he asked her sister. "I mean, we'd love to get you on camera."

"Me?" Vanessa raised her eyebrows. "Well, sure. If it's helpful." Her sister avoided eye contact. "Pali Maui was originally owned by my father, Dr. Robert Hart." Vanessa's voice faded as she took Curtis by the arm and led him away, while still talking. The camera men followed closely behind with their lens pointed.

Ava stood there, dumbfounded. She parked her hands on her hips and watched as her sister pointed out the mango grove. Before moving on, Vanessa posed for the camera again, flashing razor straight teeth that were the color of sugar. When Curtis yelled "Cut!" her sister turned back with a perplexed look as to why her sister had neglected to join them.

Ava frowned and headed for the office, rubbing her forehead in frustration. "Typical Vanessa," she huffed under her breath.

She didn't know what surprised her more, the fact that her sister had not changed, or that her antics still bothered her.

She had never needed to be the star in the family. Just the opposite. She was a successful businesswoman who didn't need anyone's approval or admiration. She was runner-up to no one. Neither did she need to stand on anyone's shoulders in order to shine. Yet, somehow, the sun had appeared in the sky—once again over Vanessa's head—leaving Ava to stand in the shadows.

25

Christel sat in bed under the covers with a half-empty pint of salted caramel ice cream and her laptop propped against her legs. She was embarrassed to admit she'd spent nearly the entire evening searching the internet. Even more humiliating was that her research target was Evan.

Katie was right. She was an overthinker.

Her neuroses stemmed from trust issues, she supposed. She'd grown accustomed to checking up on Jay. In the end, when her ex-husband's lips were moving, he was lying.

He hadn't really bought a generator for the condominium management company he worked for. When the reimbursement failed to show up, she knew. He wasn't late because he'd had a flat tire...again. She'd marked the tire in his trunk with white chalk proving that not to be true. And, no...he didn't have the flu, he had a hangover.

She had no particular reason to doubt anything Evan had told her, just the opposite. There seemed to be something he *wasn't* telling. That in itself felt like a giant red flag. She did not like secrets.

The clock on the bedside table showed the hour was far past her normal bedtime when she finally hit paydirt...a news article about the accident in Iraq. There was also a photo of a woman...Tess Marseille. She was beautiful—dark hair, pale complexion with chestnut-colored eyes. She wore a uniform and a warm smile.

The news story recounted her distinguished military career and stellar service to the nation. There were emotional interview segments from her mother and father and a brother, all revealing how the loss had affected them. The most difficult to read was the details of the accident itself.

Apparently, it had been a two-helicopter operation. As they came into Fallujah's airspace from the north, the first round of machine gun fire hit. It was later determined a machine gun had been set up on a rooftop in a village below and was shooting at them.

The helicopter teetered. Tess bravely maneuvered the craft and may have pulled out of the danger but an RPG followed hitting the fuselage so hard it sent the aircraft crashing into the ground.

Christel found herself not breathing as she read the account. She imagined the tragedy and the aftermath and it made her heart ache for Evan and all those who loved this brave woman soldier...the woman Evan had loved.

Most of this he'd told her. Perhaps the shadow on his face was not from hiding but simply the pain that came from talking about it.

She was nearly ready to close the laptop and try to sleep when something caught her eye in the last line of the article. She blinked and had to reread it.

The passenger in the other helicopter was identified as Dr. Evan Matisse.

∽

"Why didn't you tell me?" Christel asked gently, pulling away so she could look him in the eye.

Evan leaned back on his elbows in the sand. "I wasn't hiding it from you." The minute the words were out of his mouth, Evan knew he'd spoken an untruth. Guilt flooded him. This was no way to begin a relationship. One of the things he most loved about his relationship with Tess was that both of them were unafraid to reveal the deep parts, the fractures that needed cleaning up. He wanted that again with Christel.

He lifted his gaze, swallowed. "I'm sorry. That's not the truth."

A look flashed across Christel's face. Was it fear?

He hurried to explain. "Look, none of this is easy for me to talk about. The accident occurred over two years ago, yet the experience still feels fresh in a lot of ways." He paused, looked deep into her eyes. "It still hurts."

"You don't have to tell me right now." She traced her fingers down his forearm. "Not if talking about the accident causes you pain."

Evan shook his head. "No, I want to. I don't want there to be any secrets between us."

A toddler ran across the sandy white beach in front of them, chased by her mother holding a waiting towel.

"No, no, no," the tiny girl repeated while her chubby legs carried her down the beach as fast as she could go. Despite her objection to losing her freedom, her mom quickly scooped her up into her arms. "Sorry." The harried mother gave them an awkward wave and carried her daughter back to where the rest of the family waited.

Evan leaned his head back and let the sun warm his face. "I was there," he admitted. "I know you read the article, but what the writer didn't say was that the loss of Tess that day...well, it was my fault. I had a bad feeling and I ignored my gut."

Christel frowned. "Your fault? How could you possibly be to

blame? We're talking about the United States Army here, right? I'm fairly certain they don't excuse a trained pilot from her mission simply because her boyfriend has a bad feeling."

Evan shook his head slowly. He swallowed against the choking pain building in this throat. Some things were harder than mending broken bones. "It's more than that. I wanted her to stay and not fly that day. As a medic, I could have stopped it." His chin dropped. "She argued that she'd trained for that particular mission and didn't want to let her team down. Despite all my reservations, I let her convince me nothing would happen, that the ever-present danger would not raise its ugly head and bite. I folded and let her go...and she died. If I had gone with my gut, held firm about the sick feeling inside, I might have protected her."

Christel watched him intently. "Oh, Evan. Surely you know none of us holds the power of life and death in our grip." She reached and squeezed his hand. "The time of our departure from this world is solely up to God."

"Perhaps," he conceded. "There's something else. Something no one else knew, not even her family." He paused and gazed down at the sand, wondering if Christel could hear his chest pounding.

"At the time of the accident, Tess was three months pregnant."

26

Jon stood in the commercial kitchen chopping onions when Katie strode in. "Jon, what are you doing still working? Our meeting with the architects is in fifteen minutes."

He wiped his hands on a white sackcloth towel and placed it on the metal counter. "I told you, honey. I'm going to have a really hard time pulling away during lunchtime."

Katie's shoulders tightened. "Yes, I know. But I told you this was the only appointment available. I didn't want to wait another three weeks. This is that new architect on the island. He's very much in demand, and if we're going to be in the house by the time Willa starts school in the fall, we need to grab the time he offered."

Jon placed his knife back in the block. "We haven't even decided that's the direction we need to take. What's wrong with our old place? After the rebuild, it'll be everything we need. And it'll be within our budget," he added.

"You're kidding, right? I mean, Mom is *giving* us the land. How can we pass that up?"

Jon looked skeptical. "We could never sell it. Not if we build on Pali Maui."

"Who says we would ever want to?" Katie turned for the door, then looked back over her shoulder. "Are you coming?"

Jasmit Tan was an architect who recently relocated to Maui from Singapore. According to his website, his designs focused on harmony between building and site. Each project sought a poetic experience of its location—a view over a pool seamless with the ocean; a second-story open-air porch that hung among tree branches; a city apartment and roof deck from which one saw moving columns of light on asphalt in the rain.

Katie considered it a coup to have landed an award-winning professional to help create the home of her dreams...her family's forever home. She had been keeping a folder on her laptop for several years filled with images of the elements she wanted incorporated, which included a two-story waterfall in the living area. No holds barred, this house would be a showplace.

Jasmit showed up right on time. He was surprisingly young. He had messy, jet-black hair, wore a goatee and mustache and round wire-rimmed shades he never removed, even inside. If she ran into him on the street, she might think he was Johnnie Depp.

He strolled the grounds with Jon and Katie following closely behind, Katie holding a clipboard and taking notes. Her mother had given them multiple options for build sites, and Jasmit was not terribly impressed with any of them.

They had just passed the grove of coffee trees when Jasmit pointed. "That's it!" he exclaimed, his face bright with possibility. "There...on that hillside."

Jon frowned. "That steep area?"

Jasmit clasped his hands together. "Yes, the structure will meld into the hillside and will be called Ledge House. The living room, dining room, and kitchen will form the nucleus in an open breezeway strategically positioned to take advantage of the views of the ocean in the distance and the trees and landscape here at Pali Maui." He turned to Katie. "And of course, we'll have the indoor waterfall element you wanted."

He started walking, pecking his way up the incline with care. "This boulder will become a rugged companion to the house. The structure will have clean lines and be clad in Shou Sugi Ban siding, which will add to the form. The interior will be light and airy." He closed his eyes—barely visible through his sunglasses—as if imagining what would be. "The entire structure will be surrounded by a deck hung with cables with railings of glass and mesh. Nothing that will hinder the views."

Katie beamed. "That sounds perfect!" She turned to Jon who stood with arms crossed against his chest. "Don't you think, Jon?"

Her husband didn't look as on board. "What is the cost of all that? I mean, approximately."

Jasmit looked at him, barely hiding his disdain. He directed his gaze back at Katie. "Is cost consequential? Perhaps I'm not the one for—"

She immediately shook her head. "No, no—I mean, yes, we'll have a budget. But we also don't want to cut corners on this project." She gave Jon a look of warning. "Let's just see what you come up with before we worry about the financial aspects."

Jasmit seemed satisfied with her response. "Fine, then. I will have the package to you in the coming weeks," he promised.

Katie struggled to wait. Every day, she hurried to see if Jasmit's package had arrived in the mail.

When the preliminary renderings finally appeared, Katie was beside herself with excitement. "He did it!" She clasped her hands. "Jasmit captured the essence of what I was envisioning. This is my dream house. Everything about it...the clean lines and modern feel, the way the rooms are lofted and airy, and the way he incorporated so many frameless windows. It's as if our house is part of nature."

Jon held up a stapled set of bids. "Katie, look at these figures. We can't possibly..."

She waved him off. "Oh, Jon. You're not thinking out of the box here. If we scrimp, at some point in the future, we'll be terribly sorry."

Jon ran his hand through the top of his hair. "Katie, I want you to be happy with this, but the bottom-line figure...well, it's just out of our reach." He sighed. "Maybe we could negotiate?"

Katie rolled her eyes. "A man like Jasmit doesn't have to negotiate. His clients all know how fortunate they are to have someone of his caliber and talent working on their behalf. They are willing to pay exorbitant amounts." She directed her attention back to the drawings. "I don't think his estimate is that out of line."

Her position on the matter was cemented even more later that night. Jon was busy at the restaurant and Willa agreed to watch Noelle for a few hours, so Katie walked over to her mom's house to show her the house plans.

"Those are wonderful," Ava said. "Clearly, this architect is talented."

"But?" Katie prompted, hearing reservation in her mother's voice.

"But I'm wondering how Jon is feeling about all this...especially given the price tag? Don't get me wrong, honey. Normally, real property can be a wise investment." Her mother looked in her eyes. "In this case, you can't sell. There will be no appreciation to capture."

"That's what Jon mentioned," Katie admitted. "But with the land you are giving us...well, we believe that equals everything out."

Okay, so maybe that was a stretch of Jon's position, but he'd come around and listen to reason. He always did.

"Equals what out?" They turned to see her Aunt Vanessa enter the room from the lanai with a towel wrapped around her head.

"Nothing," Ava said, quickly gathering the renderings and proposal into a pile.

"I came over to show Mom what the architect has in mind for our house. I simply love the concept Jasmit came up with."

Aunt Vanessa unwrapped the towel and patted her damp hair. Suddenly, she stopped. "Wait, you don't mean Jasmit Tan?"

When Katie confirmed his identity, Vanessa's eyes widened. "We did a story on him at the station. Do you know the reputation that man has?"

Finally, someone who got it...a family member who might be totally on her side. "Yes, I do. His projects have been featured in Architecture Today. He's highly sought after."

Vanessa tossed the wet towel over the back of the sofa and drew closer. "Oh, my goodness! I can't believe you're working with him. He's from Singapore, right? He's so talented."

"And expensive," Ava added as she pulled the damp towel off her sofa cushion. "I was just telling Katie that the financial burden might be too much for her and Jon at this juncture."

Ignoring her sister, Vanessa rushed over and pulled the renderings off the counter, unfolded them for closer examination. "Look, here. See how he uses glass and natural elements... that's his trademark."

Katie and Vanessa both slid into barstool seats and buried themselves in the plans. Vanessa commented on the plan for the deck. "And look at the photos of the master bathroom. Those images are almost spiritual."

"Vanessa," Ava said.

Without looking up, Vanessa turned to another image. "And the hardware in the kitchen." She shook her head. "I can't wait to see all this finished."

"Vanessa!" Ava nearly shouted.

Both Katie and her aunt turned around. Katie's mom had her hands on her hips. "Can I speak to you for a moment? Alone?" She motioned for the hallway.

"Okay, yeah...sure." Vanessa slid from the barstool and smiled over at Katie. "Honey, I'll be right back."

Katie watched her mom and her Aunt Vanessa head down the hall. When they disappeared behind a closed door, she shook her head. "Man, what's up with that?" she murmured.

Whatever it was...from the look on her mom's face, it was anything but good.

27

"What's up?" Vanessa asked innocently. "Is there something you wish to talk about?"

Ava eased the door closed, turned and shot her sister a look. "There's nothing I *want* to discuss." She drew a breath. "Only this. On your short visit, I need you to refrain from giving advice to my kids. Especially if it's the absolute opposite of what I'm telling them."

"I'm not sure I follow. What did I do?" She seems genuinely clueless.

Ava pointed in the direction of the closed door. "Out there, in the kitchen. I'm urging my daughter to consider the financial implications of moving forward with this project so quickly. I know her. She's impulsive and doesn't always think everything through. She can be a very strong personality, and Jon often folds to her wishes. Katie can benefit from a different viewpoint...from someone she trusts and listens to. I don't tell my children what to do, but they respect my opinions." She huffed. "So, I don't need—or want—you to sweep in here and offer yours." She parked her hands on her hips. "Are we clear?"

Ava bit back adding that she didn't need Vanessa to mother

her children when her sister had done such a miserable job at raising her own daughter, but she couldn't bring herself to be that mean. She was, however, willing to get her point across. "Do you understand?" she repeated.

Anyone else might be taken back. Not Vanessa.

She smiled—a smug, assured-of-herself smile, her going-out-on-a-limb-for-no-one smile. That's when Ava decided it was time to cut this visit short.

"It was good of you to drop in and see us," Ava began. "But it may not be a good idea for you to stay. Perhaps we can book you a flight back to Seattle as early as tomorrow?" she suggested. There was no need to provide a reason. She and Vanessa had a long history. Her sister would have no need to question Ava's position, no need to wonder at the severe tension that had mounted between them.

Vanessa threw up open palms in protest. "Wait! I haven't seen all of you for so long. What's the point in—"

"There is no point." Ava's eyes narrowed. "Why did you come?" she challenged. "I mean, the real reason. Guaranteed you didn't simply drop in for a family get-together. Why are you here, Vanessa?"

Before her sister could answer, there was a tap on the door. It eased open and Katie poked her head inside. "Is everything okay in here?"

"Everything is fine," Ava reported. "Your aunt...well, she'll be going home tomorrow. So, perhaps we can have a little get-together tonight as a bit of a send-off."

Katie frowned and quickly glanced between the two of them with suspicion. "I thought Aunt Vanessa intended to stay a while." She moved into the room. "There's no need to go so quickly. Please stay," she urged.

Suddenly, it looked like Vanessa cared. Her eyes went soft.

"Tell you what—" she said, slipping her arm around Katie's shoulders. "Let's do what your mom suggests. Let's all gather and enjoy this evening." She looked back in Ava's direction. "And we'll see what the morning brings."

After Katie left, Ava went back in the house and showered. When she got out, she dressed and applied a little make-up, then checked her phone for the first time that day.

There was a text message from Alani.

"Hey, girl. Went for my routine physical this morning. The doc thinks I need to get more exercise. I promised him I would take more walks...so, you up for a stroll to Island Cream Company? I'm craving a Sposhy."

A smile returned to Ava's face. Sposhy was one of her best friend's favorite treats—made of shaved ice filled with ice cream and topped with tiny chunks of pineapple and drizzled with coconut puree. She texted back, "*Sure. Say...eleven o'clock? Why don't I meet you at Banyan Tree Park?*"

Alani quickly sent another message. "*Oh, heaven's no! I'll meet you in the Lahaina Gateway parking lot.*"

Ava rolled her eyes and typed back, "*But that's only a few feet from the front door. I'm not sure that's what the doctor ordered.*"

Alani immediately replied. "*I promised I'd walk. I didn't commit to how far.*"

Later, with treats in hand, Ava and Alani meandered outside to one of the outdoor tables. "Okay," Alani said. "I know that look. Spill."

Ava dipped her spoon into the frozen dessert. "What look?"

Alani pointed her tiny plastic spoon at Ava. "That look. You have *hopohopo* written all across your face. Worry causes wrinkles, you know."

"That's not true," Ava argued. "If it were, my complexion would look like a map of the Grand Canyon."

Alani let out a belly laugh. "Ah...yes. You've had a lot on your plate this year, much to work through in order to find your *mahulia*. You know, feeling peace is worth the effort."

Ava nodded and stabbed her frozen treat with her spoon.

"Yeah, I agree. It's just that...well, as you know Vanessa showed up."

"And you're not happy to see your sister?"

"It's not that I don't want to be happy to see her." She held the spoon midair, letting her bite of Sposhy melt. "We have a tense relationship."

Alani's eyes twinkled. "Yeah, you could say that."

Alani had been there for nearly all of it. All the times her narcissistic sibling had pulled another of her stunts, leaving Ava to clean up the mess.

The list of Vanessa's infractions was long.

One time, well before cell phones, Ava was cooking breakfast and had the phone receiver wedged to her ear talking with Mike Peterson, a boy she hoped would invite her to the year-end school dance.

Tapping her foot, Vanessa became impatient. "Get off the phone," she warned. "It's my turn."

Ava forked a strip of bacon and turned it in the pan, ignoring her sister's pleas. Vanessa was always on the phone. It was a rare occasion when Ava was on it.

She turned a deaf ear to her sister's complaints. Instead, she focused on Mike's voice. "So, I was thinking maybe you'd want to go to the dance...that is, if you don't have a date already."

Ava's chest swelled with excitement. She opened her mouth to say yes when Vanessa reached and pressed the switchhook on the wall phone. The line went dead.

Ava furiously turned and Vanessa grabbed for the phone. "My turn!" she shouted.

Ava got so angry she lost her temper. In a rare showing of hostility, she reached and yanked on Vanessa's hair. Vanessa, in turn, grabbed the front of Ava's brand-new peasant blouse, tearing the elastic and ripping the fabric down the middle.

That was it! The fight was on.

The two of them punched and pulled and screamed at each

other. Ava wasn't sure which of their arms hit the handle on the frying pan, but when the pan tipped, bacon grease went flying. A couple of steps and they both went down.

Their father immediately bolted down the stairs to check on the commotion. He took one look at his daughters on the floor wrestling in bacon grease and grabbed both their arms. After a severe scolding, he sent them to their rooms where they were grounded for weeks...well past the dance Ava wanted to attend.

Ava's gut pulled in on itself. That was only one of many such memories. In fact, every memory of Vanessa ended with Ava being hurt. Physically, emotionally, mentally. She had a lifetime of those. She'd loved Vanessa through it all, but as an adult, her sister had turned her back on family. That was something Ava couldn't excuse.

In the few hours since her arrival, Vanessa had proved her colors had never changed. She was still the same self-focused, irritating, thoughtless person she'd always been. No room was big enough to hold all her emotional baggage.

Ava liked to believe she was the bigger person...that she'd outgrown all that contention. Yet, even now, her shoulders tightened just by being in the same room with her sister. It was only a matter of time before Vanessa's true nature would erupt and cause havoc. Ava needed to protect the kids...and herself.

Simply put, Ava was done. She was no longer interested in wrestling in bacon grease.

Vanessa needed to go home.

28

Christel quickly learned her family were nothing more than a bunch of interlopers when it came to her budding relationship with Evan.

Her mom wanted her to embrace the new opportunity for love, but in her words, "Be careful, Christel. I don't want you hurt again." Katie seemed as giddy as a schoolgirl. "What was it like when he kissed you?"

The boys were less obvious. Subtle or no, they still expressed thoughts on the matter. Shane urged her to have a good time. "Go for it, sis. What's the worst that could happen?" Aiden was quick to point out the worst that could happen. "I'm happy for you, sis. Just be aware, nine out of ten relationships sink soon after they set sail."

While Christel knew they all meant well, she was determined to ignore all the ancillary advice. She was having a good time. There was something powerful in feeling wanted. She felt pretty again, and desired. She wanted to talk to Evan for hours. That said something.

That didn't stop her from pondering where all this with Evan was heading. What if things turned out badly? What if everything fell apart? The possibility broke her heart because her instincts told her she may have found a man she could fall in love with.

Evan was steady and reliable. His core never wavered. He was kind, generous, compassionate. She found him wonderful in every way. Not only was he drop-dead gorgeous, but he could make her toes tingle with a single look.

She loved how he interacted with people, especially strangers. He was a medical professional, accomplished and respected in his field. He had a great sense of humor, was a skilled listener and she knew she could trust him.

Despite all that, she reminded herself she'd been in a very similar position before, thinking herself in love.

Love was never enough.

Jay had been her everything for so long, but at the end she'd felt their bond seeping away like a slow leak. She'd tried to stick her finger in the dam but it kept leaking, leaking, leaking until there was next to nothing left but the pain wedged deep in her heart. She couldn't fix him...and was forced to let go.

After her divorce, she'd spent months doing some serious damage to containers of Ben & Jerry's. Except on rare occasions, she didn't bother with makeup or any kind of social life. It was as if someone had clipped her wings and she could no longer fly.

She could barely imagine feeling whole again. Yet, the more time she spent with Evan Matisse, the more she felt all things were possible...including falling in love.

Katie was right. She did overthink everything.

Christel snapped out of it and tied on an apron. She opened her refrigerator door and pulled out ingredients for a salad, then placed the vegetables on the counter and pulled a knife from the block. She'd diced two tomatoes when the doorbell rang.

She smiled. Evan was always right on time.

She wiped her hands on a kitchen towel and went for the door. "Hey, there you are," she leaned and accepted a kiss on the cheek. She took the bottle of wine he carried and bid him to follow her into the kitchen.

She inspected the label. "Ooh, an Ulupalakua syrah," she noted. "How did you know I was in the mood for a nice dry red?" She put an opener in front of him then retrieved wine glasses from the cupboard.

He slid onto a bar stool and ran the opener around the foiled bottle top. "So, what are you making?" Like an expert, he popped the cork.

"My signature Mediterranean Chopped Salad." She picked up the knife again while he poured their wine. "I make it often when our family gathers for a beach picnic. Tomatoes, chickpeas, cucumbers, red onion, over-chopped romaine with crumbled feta and a dressing that is to die for."

"Sounds delicious." He held up his glass and swirled before taking a sip. "Can I help?"

"Absolutely." She gathered the ingredients for the salad dressing and handed him a bowl. After careful instructions—just a pinch of salt and don't use too much Dijon mustard—she pulled two cans of chickpeas from the panty. When she turned, he was behind her.

Evan folded his arms around her waist and nuzzled the back of her neck. His warm breath made her knees go weak. "Has anyone ever told you how amazing you look in an apron?" he whispered.

"I—well, my brothers tease I look like Aunt Bea in the old Andy Griffith television episodes."

He placed a soft kiss just behind her right ear. "Your brothers need glasses," he said as his fingers caressed her cheek. "I'm getting immoral thoughts," he warned. With that, he turned and pulled her close, holding her against him. His hand slid under her hair at the back of her head and he leaned and kissed her.

She moaned. "Me, too."

"Yeah, I have a lot of inappropriate ideas running through my head right now, and while moving ahead might be just what this doctor ordered, perhaps we should—"

Christel's breath caught. "You think so?" If they didn't pull away, she knew where this would end. Part of her wanted nothing more than to give in to this moment. Another part—her brain—was flashing yellow caution lights.

"Be careful," she heard her mother say. Then Katie's voice filtered in her brain. "You overthink everything,"

"Go for it," Shane urged.

But it was Aiden's warning that tipped the situation...and the mental image of a ship sinking.

Evan had trusted her enough to tell her about Tess and the baby. What did it say that she had yet to reveal how things had unraveled with Jay...and why? Shouldn't she tell him everything before letting things go any further?

"Maybe it's best if we—" she murmured, feeling breathless. Before she could finish her sentence, her phone buzzed. She grabbed it from the counter. The text was from her mother.

"Hi, honey. We're all meeting at Kama'ole Beach. Don't be late."

29

Katie dropped the children off with her mother before heading over to No Ka 'Oi. The lunch rush was over and only a few guests lingered at open air tables. A slight ocean breeze carried the scent of tuberose and gardenia—plants she'd suggested to the landscapers when they were lining the walkway.

Like with a lot of the additions here at Pali Maui, she'd had her hand in the planning of this restaurant. She's the one who chose the blush-colored linen draping the tables and the exotic protea used in the centerpieces. It was her idea to switch out the flowers daily and to print a horticultural essay in the back of the menu. A nice touch, or so *Conde Nast* had reported in their piece on the restaurant when they featured an article on Pali Maui last year.

Marketing was her forte. She was naturally good at it. Many believed great publicity involved expensive advertising and purchased hype in the media. That was all true to some extent. Katie believed public opinion was even more paramount and could be swayed in a number of ways.

For example, exclusivity. No Ka 'Oi had a highly publicized

six-month waiting list that propelled an urgency and made island residents and tourists scramble for reservations. The next was location. The restaurant was constructed at a strategic spot looking out over the golf course and the lagoons with a breathtaking backdrop of the ocean in the distance. The food had to be unique and surpass expectations. The menu she helped develop highlighted Jon's flair for serving farm-fresh local fare, including fish pulled from the ocean waters only hours before being plated. Topped with gracious service and voila! They'd assembled an unforgettable, and highly desired, experience.

Yes, she knew all the secrets to manipulating decisions. Now, it was time to put that same magic in play for herself.

She found Jon in the kitchen giving instructions to the sous chef. Dinner would feature opakapaka caught that morning in the deep reefs of Molokai, with garlic, capers, white wine, and wild mushrooms grown by a local farmer in Hana.

When he'd finished his discussion, she cleared her throat making her presence known. "Hey, honey."

Jon turned, surprised to see her. "Hey, what's up? Did you close the Market early?"

She nodded. "Yes, and I took the girls over to Mom's. She offered to let them ride with her to the beach picnic."

Her husband groaned. "Oh, man. I forgot. Is that tonight?"

"Yes. It's a going away get-together for Aunt Vanessa." She picked up a dishcloth and wiped off a spot on the door of the walk-in cooler. "Frankly, I don't think Mom and her sister have gotten along too well on this visit."

Jon took a large pot from the metal counter and hung it back in place on a hook near the stove. "Why do you say that?"

Katie shrugged. "I can tell, that's all."

"That's a shame. I really like your Aunt Vanessa. She's interesting and funny. Did you hear her tell us about the time she arrived at the scene of a robbery with her news team from the station and there was a lady outside the bank who acted totally inappropriate?" He laughed.

"You mean the lady who kept lifting her dress for the cameras?" She raised the hem of her printed sundress and grinned.

Jon's eyes flew open. "Katie! You're not wearing any—"

"No, I'm not," she confirmed. "And the girls are over at Mom's."

In less than twenty minutes, they were over at the shanty and in bed. A half an hour after that, Jon lifted from the rumpled bedcovers. "That was...unexpected. And wonderful," he added.

Katie smiled. "I thought so, too." She traced her fingers through her husband's chest hair. "Honey, I was thinking about what you said about our architect. I've done a lot of thinking and I think I understand where you're coming from...I mean, about the expense and all."

He looked at her with surprise. "You do?"

Her fingers lifted and stroked his scrubby chin. "I do. All I want is for us to be happy. I suppose we can have these kinds of special moments in our old bedroom. We don't need bi-fold glass doors that open to an open-air deck. We don't need moonlight drifting in across the bed when I..." Her hand reached under the covers for him.

She didn't get to finish her sentence. Jon groaned as he pressed her against the sheets and covered her mouth with his own.

Katie stifled an internal chuckle and kissed her husband back.

30

Shane slowed his bike and pulled off the highway onto a gravel driveway. He coasted to a stop and cut the engine, pulled off his helmet and turned. "So, what'd you think?"

His Aunt Vanessa pulled her helmet and shook out her hair. "Loved it!" She climbed from the back of the bike and inspected his 1979 Harley Davidson Shovelhead. "Rides better than I expected." She grinned. "I may have to buy one for myself."

Shane beamed. "It's a great bike. Sure, it needs some work but I got it for a steal."

His aunt placed her hand on his shoulder. "You did good." She stared at him for a moment. "So, your mom tells me you're working with Jack?"

"Yeah." He shrugged. "It's cool."

"I seem to remember you weren't a huge fan of school. I'm glad you stayed enrolled."

He pocketed the motorcycle key. "You got that right. It all seems so stifling. I mean, how do you choose what you're going to do for the rest of your life? The world is big. I don't want to miss anything." He gave her a sideways grin. "But Mom kinda insisted. I'm no Aiden, Katie or Christel. I'm me. Nothing is going to change me."

Vanessa raised a pretend glass in the air. "To the free spirits of the world. Cheers."

Shane raised his fake glass to hers. "We rule!"

Shane took her helmet and he placed both on the seat of his bike. "So, you ready for this?"

She nodded. "Ready." She linked arm-in-arm and they walked toward a building with a neon-sign that read *Olowalu Tattoo*.

Inside, a heavy-set guy with a long mustache reclined in a chair. A tattooist leaned over the man's bicep using a buzzing rotary pen. He appeared to be shading an image of a bull dog.

A flatscreen television mounted on the back wall broadcasted an episode of *The Price is Right*. When the contestant spun the big wheel and landed on the number one hundred, the guy in the chair suddenly shouted, "That's right, man. You got it."

Shane and his aunt exchanged amused glances.

The tattoo artist quit etching his customer's skin and greeted them. "The books are over on that table." He nodded in the direction of a sitting area with a coffee table laden with binders.

Shane reached in the back pocket of his jeans and pulled a folded paper and held it up. "We have our own design."

The tattooist nodded. "Well, I'm Thor Magnum. Take a seat. I'll be finished up here soon."

When it was their turn, Vanessa went first. Shane could tell she was a little nervous, so he stood by her side for support. "I can't believe you've never gotten a tattoo, Aunt Vanessa." His mom and sisters didn't have one, but his aunt was *sooo* much cooler than them.

"My contract with the station wouldn't allow tattoos," she

told him, then squeezed her eyes tightly shut as the pen hit the inside of her wrist.

"So, I haven't seen you in here before," Shane said to the artist. "You new to the area?"

"Yup, had a shop in Sun Valley, Idaho. Closed up about a month ago and decided to chase the waves. Setting up shop near Olowalu Beach seemed like a good idea."

Shane could appreciate that. "You check out Pe'ahi yet? Some of the best backdoor around. I could take you out there sometime to watch. Warning, those waves have a lot of juice. Not for beginners."

Thor chuckled. "Yeah, I heard that. I'd love to check it out." He looked down at Vanessa who had now dared to open her eyes. "How ya doin', sis?"

She smiled back at him, obviously appreciating his physique. "Good, actually."

Shane was disappointed to learn she was leaving in the morning. Katie told him there was tension between his mom and her sister. He didn't know about all that, but he couldn't imagine the two of them at odds.

After they were finished with the tattoos, they walked over to Leoda's Pie Shop and he asked her about it.

"So, what's up with you leaving? I thought you'd hang for a while. Especially since it's been like forever."

Her expression turned wistful. "There's not a lot in my life I'm sorry about, but I do regret letting so much time pass between visits. It's been great to connect again." She held up her wrist and examined her fresh tattoo. "I love that we got matching tattoos. How did you come up with the design?"

He caught that she'd diverted the conversation. He didn't mind really. Everybody had their junk.

Shane lifted his tattooed wrist with a freshly-inked hono turtle with a wave design. "Tribal Hawaiian tattoos hold a special place here on the island. You only have to watch that kids' Disney movie *Moana* to understand how much Polynesian people give importance to their tattoos. I chose turtles because they're known to live on both land and water. It's said that symbolizes struggle."

"I like it." Aunt Vanessa stepped up to the glass counter and pointed to a coconut cream pie. "A slice of that one, please," she told the lady behind the counter. She turned to face him. "And what's your struggle, Shane?"

He shrugged his shoulders and grinned. "Everything."

SHANE DROPPED off his aunt at his mom's house then walked his bike the short distance to the shanty where he lived. The small building was a duplicate of the one Katie and her family were staying in. The structures had been built years back so the workers would have on-site housing. Most were vacant now, but his mom was reluctant to remove them. "The shanties often come in handy. Besides, they aren't in the way."

He was only yards from his front door when he noticed an unfamiliar car parked at his entrance, a small white sedan. None of his friends would be caught dead in that grandma car.

The driver's door opened and his breath caught.

"Aimee?" He threw the kickstand down and hurried over. "What are you doing here?"

He hated that he was so pleased to see her. It'd been a while, but she looked just as he remembered. He loved the way her long blonde hair flowed over her shoulders and how her spunky nose kind of turned up at the end.

He especially loved the memories of waking up next to her. She had a killer body.

"Are...are you back?" he asked, trying to hide how hopeful he felt.

Without answering, she opened the back door of the car.

Bracelets made of braided jute and beads adorned her wrist. She reached inside and lifted a bundle out, pulled back the blanket.

It was a baby!

"What the heck? Is that yours?" he asked. He moved closer for a better view. The infant smiled and drew a tiny dimpled hand into his mouth. "Wow, Aimee. I mean, holy cow."

He looked up at her. There was something unmistakable in the look on her face.

His muscles all tightened at once. Sweat broke out on his brow. "Why...why are you here?" he managed to ask.

She gave him another look...one that suggested she didn't consider him to be the brightest lightbulb in the box. "Meet Carson Shane."

Shane's heart skipped a beat. He couldn't swallow. "I don't understand."

Aimee rolled her eyes. "Then, let me spell it out for you." She looked him straight in the eyes. "He's your son."

31

Ava looked up as Vanessa entered the kitchen and immediately felt annoyed. Her sister wore a pair of tight jeans and a T-shirt. Her hair looked windblown and even though she wore no makeup, she might be mistaken for a girl half her age. Of course, she was sure her sister's natural look had been carefully cultivated.

"Did I hear a motorcycle?" Ava asked. She reached for a stack of napkins and tucked them inside the picnic basket on the counter.

"Yeah, Shane just dropped me off."

"You were with Shane?" Ava didn't know why that bothered her. She hated being jealous, but Shane was her baby. He'd never taken *her* for a ride on his bike.

As soon as the thought formed, she knew she would never have accepted the invitation. She'd likely have cited all the dangers and pummeled her son with questions about whether or not he'd used the money she gave him for a mechanic to give the bike a thorough inspection. She wanted to make sure that his used motorcycle was running properly and was safe.

That's what a mother does, she argued inside her head.

Vanessa may not realize it, but safety was paramount to a responsible parent.

Vanessa rubbed at the back of her neck. "Yeah, we took a ride to Olowalu Beach. Shane tells me those people in the tents are camping for free." She shook her head. "You wouldn't find that in Puget Sound. Every inch of shoreline is lined with luxury view homes. Even in the public spaces camping is not allowed."

Ava took a deep breath and hid the angst she felt toward her sister. No other person brought out the worst in her. Everything Vanessa said and did seemed to disquiet her and make her anxious—like there was a shark swimming beneath her feet ready to bite.

Sisters shouldn't feel this way. She felt guilty and wanted to stop...but how did you go about such a thing? Especially given her sister's narcissism.

She moved for the refrigerator and pulled out some sodas. "You might want to change clothes. We're leaving for the beach soon."

Vanessa nodded. "Yeah, that's a good idea. Hey, mind if I have one of those?"

Ava extended a can of soda. Vanessa thanked her and popped the top. She took a long swig. "Thanks, I didn't realize I was so thirsty." She ran her hand through her hair.

"Wait...what's that?" Confusion pleated Ava's forehead as she leaned forward for a better look at the reddened spot on her sister's wrist. "Is that a new tattoo?"

Vanessa stretched out her arm. "Yeah. Like it?"

For a terrible, awkward moment, they just stared at each other. "Well, it's not something I would do, but—"

"Shane and I got matching tattoos." The look on her sister's face seemed triumphant, like once again they were in competition and Vanessa was the victor.

It was the tipping point.

Ava squared her shoulders. "I'll drive you to the airport tomorrow," she said through clenched teeth. Why did this relationship always have to be so hard? She wished they could just be like other sisters.

Vanessa's eyes teared up.

"Oh, don't do that. I'm not attending that pity party."

A flash of anger crossed her sister's face. "What have I done to you this time?" Vanessa swallowed, seeming to be trying to gain control of her emotions. "Yes, my list of past infractions is long. We haven't even seen each other in nearly ten years. Is it possible I'm different now?" She lifted her chin as fresh tears sprouted. "Is it possible for you to drop those stones and quit judging me, even if only for a moment?"

"I am not judging you," Ava countered.

"Yes, you are. I see it in your eyes every time you look at me. Did it ever occur to you I might be here for a reason?" Vanessa's panic poked through. "And before you ask...I was fired. The station let me go. It appears I created quite the scandal by not realizing the mic was hot. I simply voiced my politically unacceptable opinion to my co-anchor. Unfortunately, the entire Seattle metro area heard it."

Vanessa's face turned haggard, like all this honesty was crippling. "To add a cherry to my humiliation, my contract contained a clause that allowed the station to terminate me for cause if I—" She made air quotes. *"Engaged in activities or conduct that were injurious to the reputation of the company."* Apparently, my trending on social media put them in a negative light. And it gets worse. According to my attorney, the contract also includes a non-compete clause that is air-tight. I'm prohibited from going to work at a competing station for at least a year."

This was all coming at Ava too fast. She felt as if she were suddenly in a boat that was taking on water. "I'm not sure I fully understand. What does all that mean?"

"It means I'm toast. I'll never work in my profession again. No station is going to touch me after all this." Vanessa's shoulders sagged with defeat. "It means all my perks vanished—my car, my loft condo on Elliott Bay, my personal stipend for beauty and wardrobe, and my personal assistant. I lost it all."

Ava scowled. "Surely you have some money put away to carry you through. Investments. Something."

Vanessa rubbed her temple and squeezed her eyes shut. When she did, a tear trickled down her cheek. She shook her head slowly. "Nothing. And, I—I have no place to go."

32

Aiden finished brushing his teeth and splashed some cologne on his neck. He was checking his reflection in the bathroom mirror when his phone buzzed in his pocket. He pulled it out and was surprised to see his brother's name on the tiny screen. "Hey, bro. What's up?"

There was a minute of hesitation. "Uh, hey...I need you to pick me up. I know it's out of your way, and all, but Mom and Aunt Vanessa already left for the beach and Katie and Jon likely don't have room, what with a car seat, and all."

"Sure. What's up with your vehicles?"

"My car is out of gas and my bike...well, I just need a ride."

Aiden made a sound, kind of a snort. "Sure, I'm heading out now. See you in a few." Shane's car wasn't known for its reliability. And the entire family all held their breath wondering when his recently purchased bike would start dropping bolts on the highway.

His brother was a financial wreck. If Uncle Jack hadn't handed him a job he'd be busted. Not that he worried about his lack of funds. Their mother always propped him up whenever things got really bad.

Less than a half hour later, Aiden pulled up to the shanty his brother currently called home and cut the engine. He climbed out and jogged up the steps to his brother's front door and knocked.

Almost immediately, the door eased open. His brother stood there holding a bundle wrapped in a blue blanket. Aiden raised his eyebrows. "What's that? I mean, is that a—"

"A baby," Shane said, finishing his brother's sentence. "Yeah. It's a baby."

"Okay, I'll play along. Why do you have a baby in your arms?"

Shane's tightly controlled features turned hollow. "Aimee showed up out of the blue back from California. She says he's mine."

Aiden nearly choked. "What? What do you mean *yours*?"

Shane motioned him inside. "You heard me."

Aiden's head hurt. "How can that be? Don't you use protection?"

"Of course, I do," Shane said, his voice tight. "But sometimes things happen."

Aiden was pretty sure he groaned aloud. Things didn't just happen. That bundle in Shane's arms was the product of his little brother's irresponsible behavior.

He loved Shane, but everyone knew he'd borrow money before he'd bend and pick up a nickel. He had no sense of duty, no notion of counting the cost of his actions. He seemed to think others would pick up the broken pieces he scattered.

Their dad used to say, "That boy came out of the womb wondering how he could get someone else to cry for him." Shane's lack of responsibility caused a lot of arguments between his parents. Especially when their mom stepped in the way of consequences.

Take, for example, when Shane was in—well, maybe it was second grade—he brought home a kitten from a litter someone was giving away at the entrance to the grocery store. His dad thought Shane wasn't responsible enough to care for a pet. His mother argued differently. "Lincoln, this could teach our son the very lessons you want him to learn."

His father eventually agreed. Unfortunately, less than two weeks later, Shane left the cat outside and it ran off.

Their mom hurried down to the pet store and bought a cat of the same color. She paid them fifty dollars and snuck the tiny animal home, telling Shane that the cat had miraculously returned.

Shane never knew the difference.

Aiden, however, snuck out and hunted for the missing cat night after night, eventually giving up. Although hawks and other predators were rare on Maui, Aiden still hoped the cute kitten hadn't come to a bad demise.

Aiden stood there now, trying to dredge up some words of wisdom. This wasn't a cat...this was a baby.

He glanced around Shane's living room. "So, where is Aimee?"

"She said she had some people she wanted to meet up with." He tightened his hold on the bundle. "She left the baby with me. I told her I had somewhere to go but she said I needed to have some bonding time with my kid."

Aiden leaned for a closer look. He was a cute little guy. Still, their mom was likely going to have a cow when she found out. "What's his name?"

"Carson. And it's about time for him to eat per Aimee's instructions." His brother got a panicked look as he pointed to a bag filled with baby paraphernalia. "I've never fed a baby." He held up his phone. "I tried to find a YouTube." He gave his trademark grin, but it didn't reach his eyes.

"Well, it can't be that hard," Aiden told his brother. "We've watched Katie feed the girls." He held out his arms. "Here, give him to me and you go find a bottle."

Shane looked at him miserably. "Thanks, bro. I thought about skipping out on the goodbye picnic but I didn't want to hurt Aunt Vanessa's feelings." He paused. "Besides, I'm going to have to tell Mom eventually. Better if I reveal the news with others around so she doesn't blow a gasket."

Aiden watched him dig around in the bag. "Yeah, glad I'm not you."

Shane pulled an insulated container out of the bag and unzipped it. Inside was a bottle filled with premade formula. "Here it is." Shane held up the bottle like a prize.

As if on cue, the baby woke up and immediately started crying. Aiden quickly attempted to hand off the infant to his brother. Shane pushed the bundle back into Aiden's arms. "You do it."

"Shane, quit being stupid. This is your kid."

"Yeah, you're right." Shane's voice was creaky, his breathing accelerated. "I'll do it."

As Aiden handed the baby over, a thought dawned. He stalled by glancing at the pile of dirty dishes in the sink...the counter littered with empty beer cans, then he took a deep breath and spilled the obvious. "So, are you absolutely sure this baby is yours?"

Shane guided the bottle nipple into the crying infant's mouth. The crying stopped. "The timing matches up. I have no reason to think she'd lie to me." He nodded toward a piece of paper on the counter. "There's the birth certificate. She officially listed me as the father."

Aiden nodded slowly, unconvinced. "Sure, bro. Whatever you think. If it were me, I'd check to be certain. But if you trust her..."

"I do," Shane said adamantly. "I may not like it, but the kid's mine." He glanced down as the baby wound a tiny hand around his index finger. "He is kind of cute." Shane slowly raised his head. "Aiden, I know you've always thought I lived too far on the edge for my own good. Thanks for not saying I told you so."

Aiden stepped back, drew a deep breath. By all indications, his little brother was way in over his head. Did he even realize how this was going to impact his life?

Aiden wanted to say the right things, in the right way, to make Shane understand. "Well, if you're going to be this little guy's dad, you're going to need to man up in a bunch of ways, Shane."

"True. But it's not like Aimee's going to stay. I haven't talked out all the details with her, but she hinted she's planning to head back to California. She probably wants child support." He sighed. "Like I have any to give her."

"What then?" Aiden posed. "I mean, after she takes the baby back with her?"

Shane lifted his shoulders in a slight shrug. "I haven't thought that far." He pulled the bottle from the baby's mouth. "Am I supposed to burp him, or something? I'm a little afraid I'm going to screw up here."

"Of course, you're afraid," Aiden told him, seeing the desperation in his brother's eyes. "From what I hear, that's what parenting is. From now on you'll always be a little afraid."

33

Christel hadn't expected for her life to take such an amazing turn. Only a few months ago, she woke every morning with an empty place inside. She worked long hours to hide the fact she was lonely...and scared. She had nothing to look forward to, no reason to feel excited about what the days ahead might bring...which is why she could hardly breathe right now.

"Evan, before we head to the beach, I have something I'd like to share with you," she said, after they'd finished with the picnic preparations. She took his hand and led him into her living room. "Sit down."

"Should I be worried?" he asked, with a nervous chuckle.

She slid into the sofa cushion next to him. "No, not at all. It's nothing, really. I want to be as transparent as you were, is all." She reached for his hand. "I know it was difficult to tell me about Tess...and the baby. While what I have to share doesn't compare to losing loved ones in such a horrible manner, I suffered a loss as well."

Christel fought to not break eye contact. Why did anything related to her divorce make her heart pound?

Evan gave her hand a squeeze. "You can tell me anything, Christel. Anything at all."

Over the course of the next minutes, she shared how she had met Jay and how they had fallen in love. "We went to school together," she explained. "Years later, we connected again in Chicago, when I was working in a campaign office. It still amazes me how I could fall for someone who was the complete opposite. In his words, I was the *brainiac* and he was the one who would rather chat up somebody and never open a book."

"How long were you married?" Evan asked.

"A little over four years," she told him. "During that time, I was scrambling to find my place as a career woman. I'd graduated from Loyola and passed the bar, then went on to become a certified public accountant. When Mom took over Pali Maui, she asked me to return to the island to help her manage the operations, especially the legal and financial aspects. She made me a very lucrative offer, including an ownership stake. I couldn't pass it up. So, we moved back."

"And Jay was okay with that?"

"Oh, sure. His family was here. Yet, in hindsight, that's when the trouble began." She swallowed. All this was still hard to talk about. "He didn't get along with his dad. The trouble between them seemed to escalate after we returned to Maui. My happy Jay turned sullen, something I failed to detect as I was focused on work and all that the operation required. He started staying out late at night. He was no longer easygoing. Little things seemed to set him off."

She swallowed. "Once, I left the peanut butter jar out on the counter without the lid. He went ballistic, ended up throwing the jar across the room and shattered it against the wall. When I came home and found the mess, I confronted him. He started crying." Christel turned her gaze to the ceiling. "I knew then that something was terribly wrong."

She shook her head. "I scoured the house and found a stash of pills in a clear plastic bag that I later discovered were Percocet. When I demanded answers, he said he'd been having some pain in his knee from an old surfing wound." She gazed back at Evan. "I wanted to believe him."

There was understanding in Evan's eyes she'd never seen before, a compassion that had nothing to do with pity. She found no judgment and that urged her on.

"I wish I could say I wised up quickly. I didn't," she admitted. "Instead, I did all the co-dependent things. When it became clear Jay was in real trouble, I spent days finding the best treatment program—a facility on Oahu—and fought to get him there. He went through all the motions but when he was released, all his old behaviors returned...and I knew. Often your gut tells you before your brain."

"What happened then?" Evan asked.

"For a long while, I traveled down the road of darkness alongside him. I made excuses for why he failed to show up to family dinners on time. I cleaned up after him, found him new jobs when he lost old ones and was fired. I bailed him out of jail when he got a DUI and paid the hefty fine and more to get his car out of impound. I hired him a really good defense attorney and cajoled Jay to make his court hearings. I ignored the numerous times he overdrafted our bank accounts. I did it all... became the classic enabler."

"And, then?"

"And then one day I woke up crying and couldn't seem to stop. I'd lost nearly forty pounds. I hadn't been out to dinner or had any real fun in months. I barely recognized the reflection that stared back at me in the mirror."

She gave Evan a weak smile. "Loving Jay took its toll. It was a lot of work to keep all those secrets. My relationships suffered, especially with my family. I didn't want anyone to know how bad it was. Of course, later I found out they all knew at some level."

Evan ran his finger along her arm. "I am so sorry."

Christel wiped a rogue tear that formed and now trickled down her cheek. "I couldn't imagine life without him. Yet, the Jay I'd fallen in love with and married had morphed into someone I barely knew. Jay's rapid decline and the end of my marriage felt humiliating. I graduated Loyola summa cum laude, aced both the Illinois and Hawaii bar exams. I could run profitability tables in my sleep and project earnings and profit for years in the future...in my head. How could someone who was smart and educated find herself in that situation?"

"His addiction was not your fault. You were simply loving your husband the best you knew how, learning along the way and trying to keep your head above water while your marriage was drowning. You did the best you knew to do," he said, offering comfort.

His words—his understanding—surprised and moved her. Deeply.

She had spent the past two years holding that inside, never telling anyone—not even her family—how that time with Jay and watching him spiral down had wrecked her.

"I only wanted to see the best in him, you know?" Christel sniffed. "In the end, my love was never enough to help him battle and beat the demons inside."

"Where is Jay now?" Evan asked.

"Last I heard, he had moved to Alaska. Working a fishing boat or something. He no longer has family here. His mother passed away from breast cancer and his dad took the life insurance and headed for Mexico. At least, that's what I was told. He sold the house Jay grew up in. Just as well. It's easier, I suppose, with all traces of him gone."

Evan pulled her against him, folded his arms tightly around

her shoulders. She could smell his cologne and it gave her comfort. "Life can hand out some real blows," he murmured.

He didn't say anything more as each of them sat pondering the unexpected turns life could take and how much heartbreak could result. They'd both experienced severe loss and the painful aftermath. They both wanted to find their footing and move on. Perhaps together.

Finally, he reached and brushed a damp strand of hair from her face. "I'm here. I want to be your safety net, the person who catches you when emotions throw you into freefall."

She took his hand and brought it to her lips, kissed his knuckles gently. "And I want to be yours," she whispered into his chest.

The past refused to change, yet here she was, allowing the sweet kiss of hope to consume the fears…the loneliness.

She smiled up at him. When he smiled back, her heart filled with contentment.

Joy felt as close as it ever had.

34

Ava motioned to her sister. "Help me with this table?"

"Sure." Vanessa flipped off her sandals and padded barefoot over to where Ava stood in the sand, to the left of a stand of tall palm trees. She bent and unfolded the table legs and helped Ava anchor them in the sand.

"We don't want the silly thing to tip over," Ava cautioned. "Especially when we load this table down with food." She turned and plucked the pretty pastel-colored cloth from the bag at her feet and draped it over the top, then positioned a vase of freshly cut orchids in the center. In the sand, at the base of the table, she positioned a lantern with a pillar candle. She'd light it after the sun went down.

"You sure put on a fancy picnic," Vanessa noted as she pulled one of the coolers closer.

"Perhaps, but I want this evening to be extra special." It wasn't every day Ava got her entire family to assemble for a picnic, including her brother, Jack. He'd been off-island for a few days away on business and his attendance had not been guaranteed. When Ava texted him, he was as surprised as she to learn Vanessa had showed up on her doorstep unannounced. He wasn't as surprised to learn why.

Together, they formed a plan. Ava called a truce with her sister and agreed to help her out. Jack would give Vanessa money, enough to hold her over until she could get on her feet. "A gift," he said. "I don't want no unpaid loan hanging in the air between us."

Ava would provide her sister a place to live. Vanessa would move into one of the vacant shanties, right next to where Katie and her family and Shane lived. Ava now knew why her gut told her to keep those buildings and not tear them down. Little had she expected to be housing nearly all her family on Pali Maui, even if only temporary. Having those she loved so close made her very happy. Yes, that included even her sister.

For the first time, Vanessa had changed. She seemed humbled...even grateful for her siblings support when she so desperately needed the help. "I realize I don't deserve this," she said, in tears.

"No, you don't," Ava had replied, drawing her sister into a brief hug. "Don't make Jack and I sorry."

Vanessa pulled containers from the cooler. "Wow, you have enough food for a small army."

Vanessa was right. She'd gone all out on this picnic. There were containers filled with her favorite salads, a Thai cucumber salad with sesame ginger dressing, a melon and prosciutto salad, and a mixed green salad topped with chunks of avocado and fresh blackberries. Sandwiches on thick crusty bread were carefully arranged in a pretty basket lined with a red and white checkered cloth. In addition to the sodas, she'd made lavender lemonade using one of Jon's recipes.

For dessert, she'd packed a surprise—chocolate-covered strawberries. She'd pull those out just before serving to keep the chocolate from melting. And to keep little Noelle from grabbing at them once she spotted the treat.

"What else can I do to help?" Vanessa asked.

Ava pointed to another cooler. "Could you assemble the charcuterie board? There's salami, olives, and cheese. I also packed dried apricots and several kinds of nuts."

A noise caught her attention. She looked up to see Katie and her family and Christel and Evan heading their way. Ava waved and they all waved back.

Right behind them, Jack arrived on the scene. He wore board shorts and a tropical print shirt open, revealing his ample belly. A cigar hung from his lips and he had a pair of Ray-Bans pushed up on his head.

He leaned and gave her a kiss, then turned to Vanessa with outstretched arms. "Well, come give your brother a hug." They embraced, Jack a little too tightly from the look on Vanessa's face.

"Sorry we're a little late," Katie said, apologizing. "We had to meet the architect at his office and sign papers."

Ava stopped dead. "Architect?" She glanced between her daughter and her son-in-law. "Does this mean you're building at Pali Maui?"

Katie clapped her hands with excitement. "Yes! We're moving forward with the house."

Willa rolled her eyes. "Did anyone doubt Mom would get her way?"

Jon's face turned sheepish. He gave a little shrug. "Your daughter has a way with her...words." He looked over at Katie and she giggled.

Ava glanced at her watch before urging all of them over to the table. "Don't wait for the boys, everyone. Go ahead and fill your plates."

Evan took Christel's hand and they strolled over to the table together. Little Noelle broke loose from her parents and ran over to them, wrapped her dimpled arms around Evan's legs. He laughed and lifted her up, then tickled her. She broke out in a belly-laugh. Givey barked and followed them to the table where she clearly hoped for someone to drop a few morsels.

Ava looked around and spotted the boys heading their way. "There they are," she said, relieved to see they made it and hadn't broke down on the road, or something worse.

She frowned, confused.

Shane had something in his arms. As they got closer, it looked like he was carrying a wadded blue blanket.

"Hey, Mom," Shane said. He looked to his brother for support, then cleared his throat. "I have someone you need to meet." He called everyone over.

When they'd all assembled, he lifted the blanket revealing the sleeping baby's face. "This is Carson Shane Briscoe. My son."

Ava's hand flew to her chest. "Your son?" She swallowed, hard. "You have a son?"

Jack withdrew his cigar and set his plate down. "Well, heavens above. Didn't think I'd see the day those words came out of that kid's mouth." He chuckled. "At least anytime soon."

Willa checked out the bundle. "He's cute. Who's the baby mama?"

Katie elbowed her daughter. "Willa, that's not polite."

"What?" Willa asked with a scowl. "You know everyone here wants to know."

Ava tried to erase the stricken look from her face. "Son?" It was all she could think to say.

Aiden coughed a little and gave Shane a nudge, urging him on. "Aimee is back from California. This was her little surprise."

Christel stared at her younger brother, her worry obvious. "Are you certain the baby is yours?"

Aiden gave his head a slight nod. "I brought up that same concern."

Ava lifted the baby from Shane's arms. "There's really no

need," she said, breathless. She gazed into the baby's face. "He looks exactly like Shane at that age." She couldn't help herself. She teared up as she realized Lincoln would never meet his first grandson.

Collecting herself, she repeated in a reverent tone, "Carson Shane. Welcome to the Briscoe family."

Vanessa placed her arms simultaneously around both Shane and Ava's shoulders. "Well, I know a good babysitter, if you need one."

Ava glanced up at her family all circled around. "I guess it's time I made that announcement."

Before she could get the words out, Vanessa's face broke into a wide grin. "I'm staying," she said, beating her to it.

"True," Ava confirmed at the incredulous stares from both her daughters. "Vanessa will be moving into the last vacant shanty."

Vanessa explained what had happened at the station, how she'd been let go because of a scandal. "It was a shock, for sure. The upside is my sister and my brother generously opened their arms. Going forward, I'll get to spend more time with all of you...my family."

They ate and talked for hours...until the sun faded and a multi-hued twilight blanketed the horizon. A silver-dappled moon soon appeared, casting a warm milky glow across the ocean's surface. The Hawaiian word for moon was *Mahina*. Culturally, people believed it to mean "provider."

Ava smiled to herself. Despite the hardships she'd suffered, God had indeed provided. She had her health, she had Pali Maui, and she had her family. It was more than enough.

She gazed upon her family, now strolling down the beach, locked arm-in-arm. In the distance, waves crashed on shore. Palm fronds swayed in the breeze.

It appeared her sister was back to stay. Christel had finally moved on from her hurtful divorce. Love was blooming with a handsome doctor who treasured her. After losing their home to fire, Katie and Jon were going to move their family to Pali Maui and build their dream home. Following a lengthy recouperation from the boating accident, Aiden was back to work at the station and had been promoted. Captain Aiden Briscoe...it had a nice ring to it.

The biggest surprise of all?

Shane was a father, a fact she still couldn't seem to wrap her mind completely around. Her son had a lot of growing up to do. He had a baby to think about now. With the help of his family, he would learn to be everything his son needed. Even better, she was a grandmother again.

In a wonderful place like the island of Maui, you always knew what to expect, and if you looked closely, you might see your future as clearly as your past. They all had a lot to look forward to. No doubt, the days ahead were filled with promise and wonderful possibilities.

She looked down into her new grandson's tiny face and tucked the blanket a little tighter. Another chapter in their lives was closing, and a new one was about to begin.

Ava's face broke into a grateful smile.

She couldn't wait.

AFTERWORD

Well, hey everybody—Aloha!

Captain Jack here. Kellie and I are so glad you joined us for the second book in the Maui Island Series. Boy, now—this one had some twists and turns!

I held my breath when I learned my nephew had been in an accident. Who knew his doctor would play an important role in my niece, Christel's life? She deserves someone like him. Fingers crossed, things will play out the way they ought.

My sister, Ava, continues to have her hands full with all sorts of unexpected situations—like our estranged sister showing up. Those two scrape on each other like bare knees on a shallow reef. My, how things can turn on a dime, can't they?

Talk about things turning...that scamp of a nephew has hit face-on with a situation he ain't easily walking from. I can't wait for the next book in the series to see how he handles this new parenthood thing.

And there's even more. A little tropical java finch flew by and let me in on a few secrets. Take 'ole Captain Jack's word for it—readers will not want to skip upcoming books in the series.

AFTERWORD

Besides, who wants to miss out on another opportunity to spend time on Maui?

Friends, Kellie is writing as fast as she can. Tides of Paradise, the third book, is now up for pre-order. You better jump over to your favorite retailer and grab yourself a copy.

As an added incentive, Kellie has slipped a preview in here. Keep scrolling to read Chapter One of Tides of Paradise.

Yes, I want my copy.

Make sure you also visit Kellie's website and sign up for her newsletter so you get notices when future books in the series are available.

www.kelliecoatesgilbert.com

Well, guess it's time 'ole Captain Jack gets back to the boat. I have tourists waiting to head out on a whale-watching trip. But we'll see each other soon! When you visit the island, drop by and I'll buy you a whiskey or a Mai Tai.

Mahalo!

~Captain Jack

ACKNOWLEDGMENTS

A special word of thanks to the folks at Maui Pineapple Plantation (waving to Debbie, Lacey, Mary and Ken!) These fine folks let me hang with them and see how pineapples are planted, grown and harvested.

Did you know pineapple crowns are planted in the earth by hand? The pineapples then take fourteen to fifteen months to grow. Maui is known for wild pigs and if they break through the fencing, they can eat a football field worth of produce in no time.

The Maui Pineapples are picked to order and are the sweetest treat you'll ever pop in your mouth...no, really! I had such a fun time on the tour and learned so much. You guys were so supportive of this series and my heart is filled with gratitude.

Thanks also to Elizabeth Mackey for the fabulous cover designs, to Jones House Creative for my web design, and to my editors, proofreaders and to my best-selling author friend and critique partner, Heather Burch, who made this book so much better.

To all the readers who hang with me at She's Reading, you are a blast! I can't believe how much fun it is to do those live author chats and introduce you to my author buddies.

Finally, thanks to my readers. All this is for you!

~Kellie

SNEAK PREVIEW - TIDES OF PARADISE

Chapter 1

"How could something so small create something so disgusting?" Shane held his tiny son's legs up in the air and positioned a diaper below the baby's bottom. Then he wretched. Twice.

He looked over at his mom. "Uh...I think I need some help here."

Before Ava could respond, Aimee rolled her eyes at him and leapt from the chair where she sat. "For goodness sakes, Shane. You'd better not throw up on our kid." She moved to his side on the sofa and took over. When she'd finished fastening the diaper, she snapped the light-blue onesie back in place, then lifted the infant to her shoulder and patted his back lightly. Suddenly, the baby burped, leaving a glob on her shoulder.

"Oh, gross," Shane said, turning away. "Everything that comes out smells." He wretched again.

Aimee laughed and turned to face Shane's mother and sister. "Spit-up is my new fashion accessory."

Ava smiled. "Ah, I remember."

From across the room, Katie bounced little Noelle on her knee. "Me, too. Now it's peanut butter in my hair." She laughed. "Welcome to parenthood, where going to the grocery store by yourself is now considered a vacation. And don't even get me started on labor. I was just glad I didn't poop on the table."

Shane's face twisted into a tight grimace. "Oh, please. Stop now. This conversation is taking a turn I don't want to be a part of."

The women in the room laughed.

"Oh, get over yourself," Aimee admonished with a wide smile. "You didn't go through nine hours of hard labor. The least you can do is listen with a little empathy."

"Men are such lightweights," Katie remarked. She leaned down to her toddler. "Take note, Noelle. Men are wimps and simply have no idea when it comes to all the things women have to deal with."

Noelle's dimpled hand lifted her shirt. "See my belly goat button?"

Katie rolled her eyes and pulled the pink shirt back over her daughter's bare tummy. "Honey, mannered women don't show their treasures in mixed company."

Noelle's eyes twinkled. "Me do."

Ava laughed loudly. "I think this one is going to grow up with a mind of her own."

"Like someone else we know?" Shane pulled a beer from the refrigerator and gave his sister a pointed look. "Katie, you want something?"

Katie glared back. "If you think that's an insult, Shane, I'll take it. I'm not ashamed to advocate for my beliefs and ideas. Knowing what you want and going after it isn't a character flaw." As if to punctuate her statement, she stuck her tongue out at her younger brother. "And, yes. I'll take that beer."

"So, how is the house coming along?" Ava asked, grinning.

Katie set her tiny daughter down on the floor to play. "We're only a few months from completion," she reported, ignoring the smirk on her mother's face. "And, yes. Jon and I have bucked heads a couple of times," she admitted. "For example, he wanted granite countertops that had these swirls of blue... well, the name was actually steel gray. Believe me, they were blue. The marbled pattern was atrocious and didn't begin to match the look we are going for."

"We?" Shane asked as he handed his sister a beer.

Katie thanked him. "We...as in Jasmit Tan, our brilliant architect." Her face brightened. "He has an incredible eye for design. Simple lines. Colors from nature. He detests rudimentary and dysteleological elements.

Shane raised his eyebrows. "Wow...that's some big word there."

Katie ignored him. "Jasmit often has up to a nine-month waiting list. We were very fortunate to cement this relationship when we did."

"Yeah, I bet Jon feels really lucky," Shane muttered.

"What about you?" Ava asked Aimee. "What are your long-term plans for housing? Rooming with Shane in that tiny shanty has got to feel crowded."

"It's all I can afford," Shane reminded. "Especially now that I have Carson. Do you even know what baby formula costs?" He shook his head. "And health insurance? I had to sell my bike in order to pay for that."

Aimee laid the now sleeping baby on her lap. She gently rocked her knees back and forth. "Your living space is pretty tight quarters." She turned to Ava. "I'll go back to work soon. The extra income will provide some options."

"We're hoping Aimee might be able to get her former waitressing job back." Shane ran a hand through the top of his hair "Of course, that'll mean added daycare expense."

"Raising a kid is not cheap, that's for sure...which is one of the main reasons we're cohabiting," Aimee added.

Ava sighed inside. She hated that Shane and Aimee were living together without being married. Sure, perhaps it was unfashionable to think like that in this day and age. She didn't care. Shane and Aimee had a little son. They should make a commitment.

Alani, her best friend and the local pastor's wife, thought the same and said so right to her son's face. "You can't expect God to bless anything you're not willing to do his way. His way is for a couple to covenant to *love, honor, and cherish each other...'til death do you part.*"

Ava knew from experience that vows could be broken. Still, she fully agreed with Alani and had floated her own subtle hints. "If money is an issue, I'll pay for the ceremony and reception. I could also help out with rent for a couple of months." She'd gladly lift her son's financial burden much longer, but Christel would have a fit. Her oldest daughter was a stickler for guarding Pali Maui's financial picture, which seemed to extend to Ava's personal bank accounts. Not to mention Christel, Katie, and even Aiden, had all followed their late father's belief that she often coddled Shane and failed to let him grow up.

Coddled was too strong of a word. She was his mother and only wanted to assist in whatever way necessary when he needed help. Wouldn't any mother do that?

Regardless, Shane made it clear, in no uncertain terms, that it was far too early for Aimee and him to discuss the *forever* thing. Aimee had only been back a short time. Even so, Ava hoped things would eventually head that way. Her mother's intuition told her that her son was head-over-heels infatuated with this girl. Despite his effort to hide the fact, Shane had moped for weeks after she left to pursue an acting career in Los Angeles. Ava sensed her son was finally moving on, then Aimee showed up with her surprise bundle wrapped in a blue blanket.

Don't misunderstand. Their entire family was thrilled, of course. Well, maybe not thrilled. No one wanted Shane to be blindsided. These things should happen in the proper sequence—dating, engagement, marriage...then baby.

Yet life rarely went according to plan. The best you could do, was to do the best you could do, with whatever came at you. She'd learned that after Lincoln had died. They all had.

Plan, or no...Ava couldn't help but wonder about the future. There was a lot to consider.

Ava supposed Christel would eventually marry Evan. Her relationship with the doctor seemed to be getting more serious by the day. Her daughter deserved that happiness, especially after her first marriage crumbled through no fault of her own.

Then there was Jon and Katie. Despite minor disagreements, their new place would be built soon. Fire had destroyed their former house forcing them to live here at Pali Maui in one of the buildings designated for workers...affectionately known as the shanties. No doubt, their family would be glad to have a new, more spacious, place to call home.

Her oldest son, Aiden, was now settled in his new position as director of Maui Emergency Management Administration. The risk he'd taken saving the people on that boat, and the subsequent injuries he'd suffered, had cemented the notion he was the right candidate for the job. She couldn't be any more proud of what Aiden had accomplished at such a young age. It was only sad that his dad wasn't here to see it.

As for her, she was learning to be happy. Lincoln's death and the aftermath had taken a hit on her soul. Despite all that, she intentionally grasped joy at every opportunity. Her heart was full.

And now, Shane was learning to be a daddy. She had a new grandchild to love on.

How could the Briscoes' future get any brighter?

YES! I want this book!

Available at all retailers

www.kelliecoatesgilbert.com

ALSO BY KELLIE COATES GILBERT

THE MAUI ISLAND SERIES
Under The Maui Sky

THE PACIFIC BAY SERIES
Chances Are

Remember Us

Chasing Wind

Between Rains

THE SUN VALLEY SERIES
Sisters

Heartbeats

Changes

Promises

LOVE ON VACATION SERIES
Otherwise Engaged

All Fore Love

TEXAS GOLD SERIES
A Woman of Fortune

Where Rivers Part

A Reason to Stay

What Matters Most

STAND ALONE NOVELS

Mother of Pearl

Available at all retailers

www.kelliecoatesgilbert.com

Made in the USA
Coppell, TX
20 February 2023